SAVING RACHEL

RILEY BAXTER

SAVING RACHEL

Editor: Leanore Elliott

Book Design: Wicked Muse

Cover Art: Dusk till Dawn Designs

"There is no greater agony than bearing an untold story inside you."

— ***Maya Angelou***

DEDICATION

-To Mrs. S, although you are no longer with us, your memory lives on in us daily. I never knew the impact of your loss, but I will cherish all aspects of our relationship forever. I love and miss you.

-To ALJ, it was my honor and privilege to be your spoiled little girl. You didn't have much, but what you had you freely and selflessly gave. I'm forever grateful for your love, example, and priceless memories. Every day my heart aches from not having you here to see how well my life is progressing. I love and miss you much.

-To all those that have been beaten down and beat up by physical and mental abuse at the hands of a parent, particularly a mother, this story is for you. Nobody can tell your story the way that you can but know that nobody can persevere the way that you can as well. You are an overcomer, you are valuable, and you are unconditionally loved.

ACKNOWLEDGMENTS

God, I want to thank you first, for allowing me to release hidden places and come out better, wiser, and stronger. Thank you for this gift that is still providing an escape from the things that need to be escaped.

To my husband and children, thank you for sacrificing your time so that I could continue to escape into the recesses of my imagination. Your support and love are immensely appreciated. NOBODY loves and supports me the way that you guys do. ❤❤

To my patient, understanding, and longevity having editor, Leanore Elliott, without you, my words would be ramblings on multiple pages. Thank you for making my journey smooth while guiding me with your expertise. You continue to be what I need in this journey. You inspire me to be better. Thank you for willingly taking a chance on me and never giving up on me.

To Phylicia Allen, thank you for continually supporting, encouraging, and pushing me. For not allowing me to quit, give up, or give in. I'm humbled by you.

To D.A. Young, words can't express my gratitude and appreciation of you. I love and value you, my sister and friend beyond what I can even articulate. Thank you.

To Tiffany Patterson, thank you for always being you and rocking with little ole me. I'm honored to call you friend. It all started with you, my gatekeeper.

To my beta reader, Candace Hendrickson, thank you. Taking a chance with the newbie isn't an easy task, but you do so with such grace. This one took me through but thank you for filling in the gaps and holes while appreciating the process. You continue to be invaluable, and I could never repay your efforts.

To my cousin, S.J, without you, I simply couldn't. You encourage me, cheer for me, push me, pray for me, and loved me through my hardest moments. Life is bearable because you are in it with me. I love you.

Last but certainly not least, to the readers, thank you for taking a chance on a newbie such as myself. Rachel and Dashawn were first introduced in my debut novel, *MEETING DR. FEELGOOD.* They hold a special place in my heart for multiple reasons. Enjoy. ☺

PROLOGUE

Twenty-Five years ago….

"Your tears don't move me, but I promise if you don't hurry the hell up, you're going to learn what does. I've got places to be, and your little ass is holding me up. Move. Faster. Rachel. NOW!" Thirty-six-year-old Debra Carpenter yelled to her slow-moving ten-year-old daughter Rachel Spencer.

"Don't holler at that girl like that Debra," their great Aunt Nelly rasped out.

"She better hurry the fuck up, or I'm going to beat the fuck out of her," Debra continued.

Rachel didn't want to go home with her mother and figured if she moved slow enough, her mother would just leave.

"Oh, you think I'm playing with your ass, don't you?" Debra spat.

"No ma'am, I'm coming," Rachel whined. "Even though I don't want to go with you."

"What the fuck, did you say under your breath? Repeat yourself and make it louder this time."

"Debra, leave that baby alone. She's going, be patient," Aunt Nelly said.

"Fuck patience," she stopped mid-talk with her Aunt to say, "I've got to go, and she's doing this shit on purpose. You have five minutes and then I'ma beat yo ass!"

Rachel ignored the warning even though her brain was telling her not to push this too far. In her young mind, she couldn't understand the magnitude of such a signal. She also didn't count on how quickly five minutes went.

In the next instance, her mother snatched her by the ponytail she wore and swung her around.

"Ow. I-I'm going" Rachel cried out.

"Too damn late, I told your bastard ass!" Debra screamed before she threw Rachel across the room causing Rachel to narrowly miss the edge of her Aunt Nelly's old floor model TV.

Rachel began to whimper, but the sound was cut off when her mother gripped her around the neck.

Debra started to squeeze as she yelled, "I fucking told you not to play with me!" Spit coated her face lightly. "I told your ungrateful, selfish, stupid ass to hurry up, so we could go, and you just had to test me. Well, I bet you think about this the next time you decide to defy my order you little Bitch," Debra continued ranting with a crazed look in her eyes as her hands tightened with every word.

Rachel was unable to do anything, but she faintly heard her Aunt Nelly screaming for her mother to get off her. 'God, I wish Aunt Nelly wasn't bedridden or on oxygen. She's gonna kill me.' Between Debra's words and quick pressure releases, she pleaded, "I-I'm sorry…" she struggled to get out.

Debra was unbothered by her daughter's pleas and continued choking her. "Next time I tell you something I bet—"

Before she could finish, her sister Mae charged into the house and straight for her. "Get the fuck off my niece, you crazy fucking lunatic!" Mae hollered yanking Debra back which caused the two to begin exchanging punches.

Rachel laid on the floor gasping for air. She couldn't believe that her mother tried to choke her out. She'd been feeling herself lose consciousness right before her Aunt Mae entered the house. Thank God for unspoken yet answered prayers.

Her mother was stretched across her bed as if she was the queen of the Nile and maybe in her dreams she was, but all ten-year-old Rachel saw was an unhappy woman who sought to make her only child's life miserable.

If she didn't always have a scowl on her face, she might even be attractive. Debra Carpenter was roughly four feet five inches of caramel beauty. The only problem was her attitude sucked. "Rachel, Lee isn't your dad. Truthfully, I have no idea who your daddy is. Now I'm stuck raising the bastard child that nobody including me wanted to claim."

"Oh God, why me? I didn't ask to be born, I-I didn't ask for her to be my mother either, I-I—why doesn't she love me?" Ten-year-old Rachel Spencer questioned as tears streamed from her eyes. The things her mother just said to her were some of the meanest things one could say to their only child, and she couldn't understand where it was coming from. It was as if her mother hated everything about her and Rachel was convinced that she regretted her very existence.

Her mother's words echoed in her mind, shattering her confidence and self-esteem. Lying in her bed, she began to pray, "God, it's me, Rachel, and I hope you're listening. Please keep me and help me to be a good girl so mommy will love me. I promise I'll be a good girl, if you can just make her love me…" Her eyes became heavy, and she drifted off into a fitful sleep.

Little did Rachel know the prayer that she prayed would become a mantra between her and God for the rest of her childhood.

CHAPTER ONE

Thirty-five-year-old Rachel Spencer was a woman with many positive things going for herself. She was a CFO at a successful consulting firm that fulfilled her, and she had childhood friends that turned into sisters who loved and supported her through trials and triumphs. In addition to this, she was in a relationship with a thirty-six-year-old engineer by the name of Dashawn Sanders. So how did she end up in this office, on this couch, staring at these plaques on the wall? *It's Saturday morning, I should still be in my bed or binge-watching Blue Bloods on Netflix.* She wondered how one person with so many positives could be here forced to process so many things. "Oh I'm sorry, did you say something?" she questioned looking into the eyes of the woman across from her.

"Just wondering when you were going to begin these therapy sessions as you have yet to open up with me," Dr. Hawkins probed. "For you to move on with your life, it's important to deal with the events that led you here in the first place. I would like for that journey to start today, is there a certain place you would like to begin?"

Rachel sat on the lounger staring out of the window trying to gather her thoughts. The day dreams from a couple of weeks ago had her revisiting some painful memories. Dr. Sharon Hawkins had come highly recommended, and three weeks ago, she made her first therapy appointment but had yet to say anything other than the usual pleasantries. The first two sessions she sat observing Dr. Hawkins, her awards, diplomas, her attire, and the office space.

She seemed to be very accomplished. Graduated Summa Cum Laude from Kent State University. An award for being rated second best psychologist in her field, although I'm not too sure how one gets an award for "best person to shrink you" and what does that even mean? The office had an inviting vibe with a water fountain wall backdrop as soon as you entered the comfiest maroon leather couch, and a beverage cart with various tea and coffee options.

Rachel did anything and everything to avoid talking, but now two weeks later, she felt like she was ready to open *Rachel's Box of Horrors*. "Dr. Hawkins, my life has been HELL and anything but a fairytale. While I have been functioning for the sake of others, I'm finding that cover-up difficult to maintain these days," she finished on a deep exhale.

Dr. Hawkins put her pen and notepad down, leaned back in her chair, and crossed one leg over the other. "First off, call me Sharon. You and I will be getting intimate as we process your life. Secondly, just as you've been observing me the past two sessions, I've been observing you, and although you think you've been functioning, I've seen a glimpse of the real *you* that's hiding behind the façade. My conclusion is that you aren't functioning as well as you *think* you are."

"Y-you have, what have you seen? I'm trying to appease so many people while pretending that everything is okay. Yet, on the inside, I'm suffocating. I've been having nightmarish flashbacks and I-I…" she stopped as the tears began to slide down her face.

"I've seen a woman who is holding onto things that are causing her pain. A woman who is trying to pretend as if she is with it, but if a strong wind blows, she might get blown away. I also see a woman that I believe is capable of overcoming everything but needs some guidance as to how. I'm hoping to be that guidance, the person who will ensure that you get what you need to overcome. Nobody's life is a fairytale, those only happen in movies. The beauty of this is that there is no set time to finish. If it takes us weeks, months, or years to resolve things then so be it. Rest assured, I'll be here for you as long as you need me. Now, would you like to discuss these flashbacks you're having, or would you like to discuss something else and work up to those?" Dr. Hawkins handed her a box of tissues.

"They may be too painful to begin these discussions with so let's talk about something else, and we'll work up to them." Rachel sniffed.

"Not a problem, you're in the driver's seat. How about we start with basic facts about your life? Are you an only child or do you have siblings? What is it that you do for a living? Is there a certain man in your life? Things of that nature" Dr. Hawkins questioned.

"Alright well, I'm an only child born to my mother, but she's been telling me for years that my dad has other kids. He, on the other hand, has yet to confirm it, so I'm not entirely sure about that. I'm the only child born to my mother so until he confirms it, I'm an only child. From what I remember, my parents were never officially together, and I was able to have a relationship with my dad until I was around nine years old. At that age, my mother cut all ties with him and forced me to do the same. The relationship between my mother and I has been strained since that age, but my father and I recently reconnected which pissed her off. Uh, I'm the CFO at K.M.B. Consulting which happens to be owned and run by one of my childhood best friends. Hmm, let's see, I'm currently dating a man that I met on a cruise almost two years ago. I've been trying to take my time with the relationship, but I'm worried that my issues might push him away. Almost two years, and I have yet to introduce him to my parents."

Dr. Hawkins was listening to the information provided, but the last comment caused her to look up from taking notes. "Hmm, I'll pin the other information for later but tell me about this man and why you think your issues might push him away? Uh, why haven't you introduced him to your parents?"

"His name is Dashawn and oddly, I'd thought the night we shared would be the standard one-night stand, but when he asked for my contact information to see me beyond the trip, I was eager to make the exchange…" she paused remembering a quick glimpse of Dashawn. Impressive abs that were on their way to be a solid six-pack, thick muscular legs and thighs that could hold her weight, and the tightest ass she'd ever squeezed as he stroked into her. *Hmmph, I'm a lucky fucking woman.*

…"Hey baby, I saw you come in and set this motherfucker off, would you like to dance with me?"

Rachel stared up into honey-colored brown eyes of the mystery man who approached her and her friends. He was somewhere in the six feet range, milk chocolate brown skin, bald headed with a goatee. He was also wearing an all-white polo shirt and white slacks with brown loafers. Rachel was momentarily lost for words as she returned to peering into his handsome face but then replied, "This isn't dancing music."

At that same time, the DJ changed up the music. "I think we need to switch up this music, what y'all think?" Boyz II Men started playing.

"Guess my luck just improved baby, this IS dancing music," Mr. Chocolate spoke again, "Now would you do me the honor of dancing with me?"

Rachel looked stunned, as this dude was fine. Seemingly unable to formulate any other words, she nodded her head as she stood and put her hand in his open palm.

Once they got to the dance floor, Rachel laid her head on Mr. Chocolate's chest as he began singing the lyrics of the song to her, "Nightfall, here we are…Making love histories…Sexual, natural…The feeling that you give me."

Rachel took a step back from him for a minute.

When she did, he took a step into her and gripped her tighter. "Don't run from me baby, I won't bite you right here unless you want me to."

As the song ended, Rachel looked at her friends who were intently watching them slow dance. But as soon as that song ended, When We by Tank began playing. So, they went from slow dancing to slow grinding.

Mr. Chocolate began crooning the song in Rachel's ear in a low seductive voice. He dragged out the "when we fuck" part of the song in her ear.

Rachel burrowed deeper into him.

"Baby, all you got to do is come to my room. I will make these lyrics very real for you," he promised.

Rachel felt a drop of liquid hit her panties and thoroughly turned on, she replied, "Right behind you sexy, lead the way." …

Rachel shook her head at the sweet memory that actually changed her life. "Anyway, we've been seeing each other since then. Early in our relationship, he came over to spend his first night at my house, and I had a nightmare. He had to wake me up as I was crying or rather sobbing uncontrollably. Since that incident, I have been embarrassed and unsure of how to respond to him seeing me so vulnerable. We hadn't been seeing each other that long at the time and nobody wants to deal with a woman with issues, especially before you've had time to get to know them. I don't want to get into it today, but my parents are the reason I'm lying on your couch so yeah, not ready for that conversation yet," she concluded as she picked imaginary lint from her pants.

"Ok, we'll shelve the introduction of parents for another day. Your other thoughts seem to be irrelevant regarding Dashawn, seeing as how you two have exceeded that night and have been going strong for all this time. Did you two discuss the dream or anything after that? How did he respond when he woke you up?" Dr. Hawkins inquired as she took notes.

"He held me and rubbed my back soothing me until I was able to calm down. I ended up falling back to sleep in his arms." Rachel shrugged her shoulders nonchalantly.

"Well, that certainly doesn't sound like a man that is quickly pushed away to me. I think you two need to discuss the events of that day so that you can resolve these feelings. It also appears that you might be wrong about him since he seems to still be very much invested in your relationship. Now, for you to move forward, it's going to be essential to surround yourself with individuals that want to see you whole. Who else is in your support circle since it appears that Mr. Sanders is already a firmly planted supporter?"

"Well, let's see, there's Kayla, Jocelyn, Caressa, Reia, Monica, and my cousin Charlene. Monica is new to the circle as she was added after Kayla married her brother Myles. Kayla and the other three and I met in the third grade. My cousin Charlene is my mom's sister Mae's daughter."

"Alright, duly noted and I'm sure we'll discuss them as our time goes along. Well, look at that we've reached the end of our time for today. How do you feel about the session? Nothing earth-shattering or too heavy today but I want you to prepare to dig in next time. Can you agree to that?"

Grimacing and rummaging through her mind to determine which situation she could discuss, she hesitated. "O-ok, I'll agree to that. No time like the present to dive in, I guess. This session was good for me, and I'm feeling okay. I'll see you in a week, Dr. Hawkins—I mean Sharon. Sorry, it'll take me a minute to get used to losing the formality."

An hour after her therapy session, Rachel was in her car heading home pondering her meeting with Dr. Hawkins. *Thirty-five years old and in counseling. I thought counseling only applied to crazy people.* Before her thoughts could shift or continue, her phone began ringing making her smile as she noted the caller. "Hey, cousin what's going on?"

"Nothing much, how are you? How did it go today, you feel all warm and fuzzy now?" Her cousin Charlene laughed.

"It wasn't bad I was sitting here thinking how crazy it is that my thirty-five-year-old ass is even *in* therapy. I thought only crazy people went to talk to a shrink, what a misconception that is."

"Uh, hate to break it to you cuz, but you ARE mental, crazy, special etcetera. Your ass has been touched since uh-uh, I don't know, but it's been a long ass time. I'm soooooo happy to see you're going to get it under control now." Charlene sniffled dramatically as she mocked Rachel.

"Girl bye, don't make me hang up this phone on your ass!" Rachel laughed. "What are you doing anyway other than making fun of me? Besides, our mothers are sisters, so you might need to make your own appointment with Dr. Hawkins to work out some issues. Aunt Mae might be just as touched as my momma."

"Puhlease, don't even try it with my Mom, her and Aunt Debra might be sisters, but I think Auntie D zapped the family of all its crazy. Shit, why do you think none of the family fool with her? It sure wasn't because she lived further away than everybody else. Hell, we didn't find out about the abuse you suffered until you were about to be emancipated from the foster care system. But I was calling to make sure that you're good. I wasn't sure how this session would go and wanted to ensure that you were balanced is all." Charlene stated somberly.

"Well, before we could get into any heavy stuff, Dr. Hawkins diverted it, steering us back to safe territory. So, I'm okay, I think. I'm driving home to relax and unwind with a good book which I have in abundance because my damn to-be-read pile is growing like crazy. I have *Meant to Be*, ooh those damn Townsend men make me clutch my pearls and pray for forgiveness for the frequent wetness of my panties. Then I have *Dmitry's Redemption*. I love a good mafia story. Anyway, I plan to chill out and read until my eyeballs begin to cross.

"Did you say you were going home to read while sounding like you're seconds away from orgasmic release? Where is that tall drink of chocolate milk you've been sweating your sheets up with?" Charlene inquired.

"Uh, maybe. Besides, his damn name is Dashawn to you and he's none of your concern. Where your man at why you all up in my business asking about mine?" she fussed.

"His ass is in my room stretched out snoring. I fucked him so good, he was out like a light minutes after." Charlene laughed.

"First of all, TMI heifer TMI. Secondly, you are a damn fool girl. I'm pulling into my driveway. Chat later, love you crazy."

"Don't hate, take notes and emulate boo. Love you back. Chat later." Charlene giggled.

By early evening, Rachel laid on the couch trying to get into the book open on her Kindle and fighting sleep. Before she could drift off, her phone buzzed displaying Dashawn's picture. "Hey honey," she purred into the phone.

"Hey, my day hasn't been complete because I haven't had my daily fill of you. Were you busy? How did your session go today?" he inquired.

"Never too busy for you, just lying on the couch trying to convince my eyes that we're reading. Um, the session went well I suppose. Everything good with you?"

"You sure about the session? Your answer sounds pretty vague to me. I also called because I thought we could go out to dinner and a movie tonight. I thought we could get our Wakanda on as the theatre is running a special weekend viewing. You up for it?'

"Sure thing, that's so cool seeing as how it topped box office charts for weeks, what time should I be ready babe?"

"Uh, be ready in an hour? I'll see you shortly love."

CHAPTER TWO

Dashawn placed his phone on the charger after Rachel agreed to a night out and walked to his closet to pick out something to wear as his mind wandered. *I wonder how her session honestly went today and if she got any closer to opening to her counselor.* Almost two years ago, he took a cruise vacation and met the brown skin bombshell that caused him to evaluate his stance on temporary and long-term relationships. Sure, he could have just brought her back to his room overnight but something about that night changed the course of his life. It wasn't just the way she twerked on the dance floor or how her hips moved when she swayed to their first dance it was in the way she held him afterwards. Then she looked at him in a way that made his heart beat a little faster and every time she grabbed and released him throughout the night, he had thought of holding on to her just a little tighter.

Shit, it even shocked him when he asked for her contact information to continue seeing her beyond the cruise, but something about that woman made him want to explore a long-term relationship. "Hmm, I'm still exploring with her," Dashawn said out loud to himself. His phone rang bringing him out of his musings. "Hey man, what's up with you?" he grumbled into the phone to his best friend.

"Nothing, Shauna just left my crib, what are you getting into tonight?" Ronnie asked. "Are we hitting the court for some hoops or torturing ourselves at the gym in the morning?"

"Man, I'm about to get dressed and go pick up Rachel, we're going to see Black Panther then going to dinner. Which option are you interested in tomorrow? I'm good either way."

"Guess I'm second fiddle again. Alright, let's hit the basketball court close to you then, I'd rather play some ball than deal with an early morning session at the gym."

"Damn straight, call Shauna with that punk ass whining. I'll meet you on the court at eleven just in case it's a late night. I'll holla at you later bro," Dashawn stated as he hung up the phone.

An hour or so later, Dashawn knocked on Rachel's door but could only stare at her when the door opened. *Gotdamn, bronze skin, double, shit maybe even triple D breasts, legs that bow with a slight gap in_them, mid-length full naturally curly hair, the cutest pudgy stomach that she hated, but of no consequence to me. Yeah, beauty should be her middle name.*

His woman was beautiful with her short ass coming to his middle area. She stood in the doorway smirking at him wearing an all-black jumpsuit that dipped deep in the front making her large breasts mouthwatering. The light makeup she wore caused him to appreciate her bronze skin and bright brown eyes even more.

As he continued to stare, her face split into a broad smile displaying straight white teeth. Tonight's attire was undoubtedly opposite of the outfit she wore the night of his first introduction with her. *Body hugging all white dress that barely came to her thighs and super high multi-colored heels.*

As an engineer, his work life kept him busy, and the cruise destination was his way to get away to recharge. He'd met this brown skin beauty because of that vacation. While he wanted to believe it would be a one-night stand, he learned it would be anything but. "Hey love, I'm sorry. You ready to go?" he asked leaning down to kiss her.

"I was wondering if you were gonna say anything or continue to stare at me. You like what you see?" She smirked returning his brief kiss.

"Do I? Shit, I'm almost tempted to walk you back until we reach that big ass comfy bed in your room," he replied.

"Uh huh, nope not wasting the makeup or the outfit now that I have them on. I'm ready, let's go. Wakanda awaits boo," she taunted.

Fifteen minutes later, Dashawn parked in an available spot at the theatre where Black Panther would be starting within thirty minutes. Watching the people decked out in various outfits gave him a sense of pride. "Alright, Rachel let's get in here. You want anything from the concession stand?"

Rachel had also been observing the crowd and laughed at some of the get-ups she saw. One guy wore what looked like the lion head coat from the movie, *Coming to America,* and he was more of James Earl Jones the crackhead addition than the father from the film. His clothes were too big and hung loosely from his body causing her to laugh. "I'm sorry babe. I can't believe that after all this time these folks are still dressing up. But what did you say?"

"Yeah, me either. Can you not be so obvious though? I don't want to have to fuck somebody up tonight because they can't handle your humor over their failed attempt at being the King of Zamunda. I asked if you would like anything before we go inside?" he smirked also referencing the movie *Coming to America* as he tried not to encourage her teasing of the guy who stood diagonally to them.

"Yes babe, I want some nachos they should tide me over until we go to dinner," she expressed with mirth in her eyes.

"Alright, nachos it is."

Nearly three hours later, Dashawn was staring at Rachel across the table remembering her entrance into the ship's nightclub. That night, her white dress barely left anything to the imagination, and he had to approach her before some other guy did. Asking her to dance was one of the best decisions he'd made on that cruise. As he held her in his arms, he became temporarily stunned by the encounter. She gazed at him with captivating brown eyes filled with barely contained desire and a hint of hidden torment. In that moment, he knew he had to have her long-term and it led them to where they were now. "I'm sorry, what?" He blinked coming out of his brief walk down memory lane.

"This is the second time you've spaced out on me tonight, is there something on your mind?" She smiled at him.

"You, only you. Just thinking about how we met. I enjoyed that night and every night we've had since." His eyes shone with a mixture of love, desire, and repressed need.

"Well, if you keep looking at me like that you're gonna get what you're asking for," she challenged.

Waving over the waiter, he requested the check. "Challenge accepted, Rachel, challenge accepted. Now, let's get the fuck out of here." Standing, he came over to her and kissed the comeback from her.

A few minutes after he was driving, Rachel placed her hand on Dashawn's lap and slowly eased herself over to her prize. Gripping him through his slacks, she felt him throb and rise beneath her hands. She slowly opened and closed her hand a few times, enjoying the feeling of his awakening.

"Unless you plan on finishing what you start in this car, I suggest you let go," Dashawn grunted out.

Deciding to indeed finish what she started, Rachel proceeded to unzip his pants freeing his cock from the confines of his briefs. Leaning gently over the console, she lowered her head and slowly moved her tongue up and down his pulsating cock. "Mm, I think I still need dessert," with that, she swallowed his dick, gagging slightly when it hit the back of her throat.

"Gotdamn Rachel!" he sputtered, gripping the steering wheel so tight his knuckles turned white as he tried to control the car.

Rachel continued sucking deeper, tasting his pre-cum fueled her need to keep going in her effort to get him to lose control.

"Shit! Unless you want me to wreck, I need you to let my man go Rachel," Dashawn pleaded.

Instead of responding, Rachel sucked him harder leaking some of the saliva collecting in her mouth. "Mmm," she moaned grabbing his balls as she added more suction with her mouth.

"Any moment now, we're gonna be beyond the point of retreat, come up baby," he grunted.

Rachel tightened her suction with such force that Dashawn's cum shot quickly down her throat. Swallowing every drop, she peered up at him licking her lips. "Now Babe that was the precursor for dessert. So – drive faster."

"Fuck, hold on," he forced out as he pushed down on the accelerator, increasing his speed.

Rachel sat in her office staring at the figures on her monitor thinking about her Saturday night. Dashawn had made her pay for her stunt in the car, and the reminder caused her to clench her thighs. *Damn, that man.* With the need to change her wayward thoughts, she decided to venture down to Kayla's office. "Hey Megan, I'll be in Mrs. Feelgood's office. I have my phone if you need me," she told her assistant. Kayla was her boss and best friend. Just before reaching Kayla's office, her cell phone started ringing, but the caller wasn't someone she wanted to entertain, so she let it go to voicemail. Not even two seconds later, the ringing started up again. Ugh, she's persistent today, she thought as she entered Kayla's office and answered the call. "Hello?"

"So, I'm guessing you didn't want to talk to me since you sent me to voicemail huh?" Debra questioned ignoring pleasantries.

Trying to diffuse the aggravation as well as avoid confrontation while at work she lied, "Sorry Mother, I didn't get to it in time. How are you today?"

"Yeah right, whatever, I need you to come over to my house and get the stuff you left in the attic. I'm about to do some renovations and can't deal with your junk along with everything else," Debra spat ignoring another pleasantry.

"Uh, ok. I didn't know I had anything there or that you were doing work on the house. Is everything ok? When would you like for me to come over and grab my things?" she questioned ignoring the jab about it being junk?

"When the hell do you think I want you to come over – today? Don't be asking me any dumbass questions either. I'm your Mom, and I don't report to you like that lackey in your office. If you're not over here today I'm throwing all of that shit away," she growled and then disconnected the call.

For a couple of minutes, all Rachel could do was stand immobile in the spot she was in. Her mother was a force, and it seemed as if every conversation she had with Rachel was laced with bitterness and resentment. When would this situation change? *When you change it,* her subconscious answered. She wondered if her life would get better regarding her mother then she remembered where she was at. “Uh, hey Kayla,” she greeted on a deep sigh her mother’s call making her forget what she came down here for.

“Everything all right with Ms. Debra?” Kayla inquired with raised brows.

“Yeah, yeah I have to go over today and grab some stuff I left at her house. I guess she’s having work done and doesn’t want my things there while it’s going on.”

“Oh ok, you want me to come with you to help you load the stuff up? I can leave Maisha at daycare and have Myles pick her up,” Kayla offered.

“No, no that’s ok. I’ll go over there and get it. The funny thing is I don’t remember leaving anything there…” she trailed off trying to remember just what she left at her mother’s house. She hadn’t lived with her mother since she was thirteen having gone to a foster home a month after her birthday. She needed to change her thoughts before she was forced to go down another dark road of her past. “So, how is my God baby? You want to go grab some lunch?”

“Uh, Maisha is good. Yeah, let’s go grab some lunch,” she cautiously replied.

Thirty minutes later, Rachel and Kayla sat in a nearby Chipotle eating, but Rachel’s thoughts were consumed. Feeling someone looking at her, she peered up at Kayla’s concerned eyes on her. “Why are you looking at me like that? Did I miss something you said?”

"You know that I'm here for you right?" Kayla reminded her. "If you need or want to discuss anything, I can be a listening ear."

"I know you are and I appreciate it. I'll be okay. I just need to process the things that are bogging down my mind." She sighed.

"Ok, no pressure. Were you able to get that spreadsheet figured out?" Kayla asked as she skillfully steered Rachel away from the current topic.

CHAPTER THREE

Later that evening, Rachel knocked on her mother's door dreading what awaited her on the other side. Preparing to knock again, the door whipped open to the face of her angry mother. "Hi, Mom. I'm here to grab that stuff."

"Is there a reason you didn't you call first?" Her mother sneered.

"Oh, I'm sorry I—uh. If now isn't a good time, I can come back," she said as she waited outside of the door.

Her mother had yet to move aside or invite her in. "Hell no, I'd rather deal with your ass now and get it over with. But don't take too long I've got things to do," with that, she stood to the side with her hands on her hips.

Well damn, so much for a proper welcome. "Uh, sure thing, I'll get it and be out of your hair."

"Wish your ass would have never entered me, fuck my hair," Debra grumbled not so quietly.

As Rachel made her way to the attic, she stewed over her mother's words and actions. *I don't know why I continue to let her get to me. Shit, she's been doing this my whole life and I don't know why I haven't become immune to her funky ass treatment. Wake up Rachel, this is your life with her, and it'll always be this way so deal with it,* she chastised herself as she looked around the attic. None of the boxes looked familiar to her she would need to ask her mother. As she turned to head back down the steps, she saw her mother perched against the wall surveying her every move with crossed arms. "Oh shit, Mom you scared me!" She jumped. "Which of these boxes belong to me?"

"Fuck if I know, aren't those yours?" Debra pointed to a couple of boxes by the back window.

Rachel walked over and peered in the first box noting the contents of it. "Uh mom, these are baby items I don't have any kids."

"Yeah I know it's your crap from when you were a baby your grandmother wouldn't let me get rid of it. I think the box next to it is yours too." She glared shooting dangers at her.

Not wanting to push her anger further, Rachel proceeded to look in the other box and noted clothes that she owned before she went to her first foster home. She couldn't believe that her mother had held onto the stuff all this time. Looking down at the old clothes caused pain as none of the items resulted in fond memories. Instead, they reminded her of the pain of her miserable ass childhood she would be dropping all of it in the first dumpster she came to once she left. Unable to form words, her phone began ringing, and Dashawn's handsome faced appeared on the screen. "Excuse me, Mom. I need to get this."

"What else is new? Everybody but me is a priority in your life," Debra spat before stomping down the steps.

"Hey Baby, how are you?" Rachel asked Dashawn answering before it went to voicemail as she tried inflicting excitement in her voice.

"Hey Love, just called to—uh, is everything all right?" Dashawn inquired sensing something amiss.

"Yeah, yeah, everything's fine," she stated trying to perk up.

"I don't believe that at all. I'll swing by your house around six thirty. See you then," Dashawn stated before hanging up.

Shit. Rachel grabbed the two boxes heading back down the steps. When she walked into the kitchen and saw the stern, angry face of her mother, a feeling of dread came over her.

Her mother's next words confirmed that this night would be anything but pleasant, "You need to remember when you pretend as if I'm non-existent in your life, that your life is a privilege courtesy of the man above of. I never fucking wanted to have you, if it were up to me, your ass wouldn't exist. Lord knows, I tried to kill you when I was pregnant, but the only thing I managed to do was abort your twin," Debra spat with cold, hard, and flinty eyes.

Rachel stiffened as her body became instantly rigid. *Did she say what I think she said?* She stared at the hateful look on her mother's face, confirming that she had indeed said those foul, hurtful words. Pinching her lips tight to keep them from trembling, she said, "I-I gotta go Mom," she stammered turning quickly towards the front door.

At six thirty that evening, Dashawn knocked on Rachel's door, something in her voice earlier made his need to check on her essential. When she opened the door with tissues in one hand and her phone in another hand… he knew his suspicions were accurate. He stepped inside, closed and locked the door, then followed behind her as she made her way to the living room. *What the fuck!*

"I'm sorry—no one. Please don't say that. Yes. No. I know, don't feel like that," Rachel said as her voice quivered.

Dashawn stood just inside the living room watching Rachel pace back and forth. *What the fuck happened and who is she talking to.*

"Please don't say that I love you Mom," she sobbed into the phone.

Dashawn couldn't keep standing by watching this conversation spiral out of control, so he walked towards Rachel and softly encouraged her to end the call. "Why don't you call your mom back Rachel? Tell her, you have company," he whispered in the ear unoccupied by her phone. But Rachel hadn't acknowledged him or made direct eye contact since opening the door.

Suddenly, she dropped to the floor crying hysterically.

What the fuck? He grabbed the phone to give her mother the what for but was met with dead silence. *Motherfucker.* "What's going on, Baby? What did she say to you?" he roared with flaring nostrils.

"I-I-I can't…." Rachel cried over and over.

"You can't what Love, you can't what?" he asked her. *How much time could I get from killing her mother's ass and pleading guilty by way of reactive temporary insanity? I'll even invent a new condition. This is fucking bullshit.*

"Oh God, oh God" she sobbed not responding to him or his questions.

Hate is such a strong word, but damn, her mother is making me consider it. How in the fuck, can she not feel any guilt for what's she's doing to this amazing woman? "Talk to me." He continued to feel angrier with each passing minute. He wasn't sure what had been said to her over that damn phone, but he knew whatever it was had pissed him off. *If I run into that woman, she'll regret tonight's fucking encounter. Focus on your woman right now.* "Come on baby." He picked her up and walked to her bedroom.

Rachel had been replaying a portion of her mother's words over and over, and they were wreaking havoc on her mind. Laying in Dashawn's arms, she had another flashback.

Mommy, why won't you let me see my Dad or call him? I miss him," Rachel whined. In her nine-year-old mind, she couldn't understand her mother's reasoning. Rachel should have just left it alone and went back to her room, but she wanted to know.

"Because I said so, you do not see his ass anymore, and no you can't call him either so stop asking. I'm sick

of you putting his punk ass on a pedestal for nothing. Trust me when I tell you, he doesn't deserve that shit. Now get your little ass out of my room before I give you something to cry about."

Rachel left her mother's room feeling like her world was crumbling. I want to see my daddy. Entering her room, she dove into her bed, burying her head under her pillow crying hysterically.

Rachel hadn't realized that she fell asleep or had been crying until her mind connected with the concerned voice of Dashawn.

"Wake up baby. Rachel. It's just a dream, wake up Love." Dashawn shook her. He had heard her whimpering but wasn't alarmed until she began crying harder. "Come on baby, wake up," he soothed her as he began caressing her back. As Rachel came awake and gripped him so tight that her nail print would be left, he fought his anger for the woman responsible for her agony.

With tear-filled eyes, Rachel looked up at him. "I'm so sorry, honey. I know this isn't what you expected when you came over here tonight," she wept wiping her eyes to stop her continued tears.

At first, all he could do was stare at her. He just couldn't believe her feeling like she had to apologize. "First of all, I'm not sure why you're apologizing. Secondly, I love you Rachel, and a part of my love means that in whatever capacity you need me, I avail myself to you. Now, do you want to talk about what happened or do you want me to hold you?" he questioned as he repositioned them in the bed.

"It started when my mom called me at work today and then she escalated as the day went on," she began as she gave him a recap of the things that had been said throughout the day.

"That bitch. I'm sorry love, I know that's your mother but her ass sure the fuck isn't acting motherly. So why should I care about her? This pisses me the fuck off. Have you discussed this shit with Dr. Hawkins?" he grumpily inquired.

"Not yet but I will. For now, can you just hold me?" She sighed into his chest.

"Anything you need love," he told her. "I'll give you any and everything you need for the rest of your life, no worries I got you."

CHAPTER FOUR

The following Saturday, Rachel laid on Dr. Hawkins lounger staring up at the ceiling as if it held the answers to all her problems.

It had been a rough week, and she wasn't sure where to begin after Dashawn woke her from yet another nightmare.

"Rachel, while I'm sure you could lay here all afternoon, I think there are some things that you need to get off your chest. I'm here to help you, what's on your mind?" Dr. Hawkins asked.

"Ok, since our last session, something happened and I'm not quite sure how to proceed. Some people might even question why I don't just cut ties and move on. But it's not that easy for me," Rachel stated as she exhaled a long breath.

"I'm not sure that I have a clear understanding of what you're talking about or who you're talking about. You want to slow down and bring me up to speed?" Dr. Hawkins expressed with raised eyebrows and confusion etched on her face.

"I'm sorry. My mother is the reason why these sessions are warranted. She has spent most of my childhood and now my adult life demeaning me, making me feel substandard, unwanted. You name it and she's made me feel it." Rachel went on to fill Dr. Hawkins in on what had taken place recently with her mother.

"Did you say that you haven't lived with your mother since you were thirteen? I'm sorry, I need a little more background."

"I mentioned that my parents split when I was nine, and it ultimately turned my world upside down. It's also the point when my mother began to express her frustration and aggravation with me. Well, shortly after I turned thirteen, I could no longer take the mental and physical abuse, so I ran away. Do you know my mother didn't even come looking for me? I was gone for three days before she did anything, and she only responded when the school truancy officer came to the house. Her response was, 'I don't know where her little ass is but I'm showing her that if she wants to be grown then have at it. And she slammed the door in the man's face. I had been at my friend Angie's house who lived across the street so unbeknownst to my mother, I had heard and seen the whole exchange. And before you ask, Angie's mom had no idea that I was there I'd been hiding out in her room, and we managed to escape her mother for three days. But that soon came to a head when Angie's mom caught me sneaking into the bathroom. Long story short, that's how I ended up in Children Services."

"So, what happened that you ended up in Children Services?" Dr. Hawkins probed. "Why didn't any of your relatives take you in, so you didn't have to end up in a stranger's home?"

"Well, Angie's mom took me down to Children Services to report on some of the things that my mother had done, and once they got involved, it became complicated. Once they notified my mother that I was with them, she went ballistic. She wanted to know how I ended up there and they were obligated to tell her where I had been. When she went home, she went over and confronted Angie's mom. My aunt Mae and my mom got into it before I ran away, so I didn't want to tell any of them what was going on. When they began questioning me about relatives, I lied and told them that my mom was an only child and that my grandparents were dead. When they interviewed my mom, she surprisingly confirmed my lie, so I had to go to a foster home. I guess she called herself, further punishing me. Anyway, that first home was horrible and caused me to have nightmares. My foster mom was mean as hell, and I should have known something was up when I arrived. Two of the girls ran away about an hour after I was introduced to my room. I cried myself to sleep that night wondering how my life continued to be such a horrible nightmare. So yet again, Dashawn had to comfort me after a nightmare last night. I wonder how long this man is going to deal with me and my issues." Rachel sniffled as she returned to the present.

Dr. Hawkins handed her the box of tissues. "Rachel, the fact that he continues to be there for you despite your *issues* says that he's serious about you. Men who aren't invested in a relationship wouldn't continue to show interest. You're gonna have to trust him to be the man in your life that you need. Is there something else you want to discuss today? I think it's a good place to stop, but if you want to dig deeper we can, it's your call."

"No, you're right, and I'm feeling pretty emotionally open. Let's wrap up for today," Rachel concluded with her red face and puffy eyes.

Two weeks later, Rachel was cleaning her desk to leave for the weekend when her cell phone rang with an unknown number. "Hello"

"Hey Chelly, how are you?" a man replied.

"Dad?" she inquired.

"Yeah Chelly, it's me. How are you? I got a new phone and number, so I'm sorry I haven't called you before now. I had to restore my other phone to get your number," her father told her.

"It's good to hear from you, Dad. I'm doing um… I'm doing ok I guess," she hesitated.

"What's going on, Chelly? I'm sensing something in your hesitation."

"Um, I wasn't expecting your call is all. Can I give you a call when I get in my car? I'm in the process of leaving work."

"Sure thing Chelly, I'll be waiting," he stated before hanging up.

Rachel was pondering how to approach the conversation with her dad, her mother's words were still bothering her, and she wanted his perception on things. She also wanted to find out how things were when the two of them were together. Her mother's actions lately were causing her to believe that maybe something happened that she was unaware of. Leaving her office, she decided to ask the nagging questions that she had. No sense in allowing things to continue to fester. Just before calling her father back, her mother called. *Damn, did she pick up my wanting to find answers?* "Hey, Mom."

"So, I'm assuming that you *forgot* to call me last night? Ever since that girl had that baby, you've been distant with me. You better not be getting any ideas because the LAST thing you need in your life is a baby. Besides, supposedly your *sister* has a few you can borrow, ask your *Daddy* the next time you talk to him. Oh, but then I'm sure he hasn't even mentioned the two kids he had on me," Debra taunted.

Then the line beeped with Lee's new number, "Uh Mom, my Dad is calling on the other line do you mind if I call you back?" she asked hesitantly.

"Oh yeah, take his call but don't forget to ask him about his *other* kids," Debra teased in a sinister way.

"Hi Dad," Rachel said answering the line before he went to voicemail.

"You sound funny Chelly. Do you want to tell me what's going on? Is everything ok?" Lee inquired.

Taking a deep sigh, Rachel decided to have the long overdue conversation with her dad. She needed to try and understand why her mother was treating her this way. "Mom has been saying some things to me since you two split up when I was a kid. Her treatment, as well as her anger towards me, has escalated since we've reconnected…" she trailed off.

"I'm sure that this isn't a conversation that you and I need to be having over the phone. I was calling to see if you wanted to go to dinner. Based on what you're telling me, I think that maybe I should come to your house. I can bring dinner, so we can eat and hash some things out. How does that sound?" Lee asked.

"I think that is a good idea. I'm on my way home now. I was going to stop and see Kayla's baby, but I think this is more important today."

"See you in a little bit," Lee said before hanging up.

An hour later, Rachel and Lee were sitting at her kitchen table eating tacos from Chuy's. "Ok, can you tell me what Mom's issue is? For starters, what happened to you two? She also says that I have siblings that I don't know about, is this true?" Rachel jumpstarted the conversation.

"I'm sorry if your mother has been treating you badly. We ended because of several things. What she won't admit is that she was cheating on me and I found out about it. I had been working two jobs, and some of the neighbors were talking. I got wind of the conversations and decided to call off work from my second job one night to see what was going on. I left home as usual but only went a couple of blocks away from the house. Roughly, forty-five minutes later I came back but parked a little way from our house and just sat there. After fifteen minutes, I was starting to think that I was crazy and maybe the rumors were just that. Then I saw one of the neighbor's brothers walking from their house and quickly moving toward our house. Based on the late hour, I knew you would be asleep and I'm sure so did your mother. Anyway, the guy was met at the door by your mother in a pink silk kimono. It was one of my favorites, anyway, he entered the house after kissing her passionately. It took everything for me to sit there and watch without moving, Chelly. I sat dumbfounded, feeling as if my eyes had deceived me. After twenty minutes passed, I drove up to the house and parked in the driveway. Then proceeded to the house and what I heard as I stepped in caused my blood to boil. Your mother was making no secret of the events that were taking place in our bedroom, in the bed she shared with me. The only thing that I was grateful for was your ability to sleep like a bear because you never woke from the noise and believe me I checked."

Rachel sat listening as he paused. Feeling a bit sick to her stomach.

"Instead of confronting her about it, I quietly backed out of the house…well, after I made a recording of her calling his name. Then I went to your Aunt Mary's house until it was time for me to get home from work. After that incident, we began to argue a lot because I was unable to hide my disdain for her. The arguing is what she believes led to our ending but right before I packed my bags, I confronted her with the recording and she was speechless. Oh, and she tried denying it, but the evidence was there, and she was busted," Lee angrily finished.

Rachel sat there stunned and unable to speak for a minute. "How could you walk out the door, recording, or no recording? Then-then-then, she told me that you cheated on her and—and…" she trailed off.

"You are the reason that I had to pull my shit together and only record the events. BELIEVE me, I wanted to storm in that room and blow shit up. As for the claim that I was cheating, bullshit and lies is my response. Before your mother and I became serious, I was seeing another woman, and shortly after your mother and I moved in together, we learned that the woman was pregnant. Coincidentally, two months later your mother found out that she was pregnant with you. After she and I split, the other woman and I got back together then we had another child," Lee concluded not meeting Rachel's eyes.

"Wow, talk about being the topic of a recorded song's lyrics?" She laughed. "But seriously, I have two siblings that I haven't met. Why haven't you ever told me about them? I mean we reconnected last year, you could have mentioned it."

"When your mother found out that I had gone back to Denise she forbid me to see you. I never got an opportunity to inform you of your siblings because she refused any access to you. When we reconnected, I could never broach the subject, and I wanted us to restore our relationship before adding more obstacles for us to overcome. Even though she cheated on me the fact that I returned to Denise after we split caused your mother to become resentful. However, you have a slightly older sister named Nisha and a younger brother named Nate. They have been anxious to meet you," Lee concluded looking at Rachel with hopeful eyes.

Before Rachel could reply, her phone started sounding with the *Halloween* movie theme song that Michael Myers was known for.

"Uh Chelly, whose ringtone is that? That's pretty messed up." Lee chuckled.

"Hi Mom," she answered unbeknownst to her hitting the speaker button downplaying the emotions she was feeling.

"So, did that bastard finally tell you about your illegitimate siblings?" Debra questioned.

"Well damn Debra, that's what we doing now? I got your damn bastard, and my other kids are not illegitimate!" Lee shouted at the phone.

"Motherfucker, I know your lame, limp, dick ass ain't talking to me. You lost all fucking rights to speak to me when Rachel was nine gotdamn years old. You put this punk ass bastard on the phone, Rachel? Don't forget that while his bitch ass was out making more fucking kids, I was raising your ungrateful ass!" Debra hollered.

"You might want to chill with that bullshit you're spewing right now, cause I'm not one to deal with the fucking nonsense you are beating our ears up with. If you got a problem with me, then you need to deal with me don't take your shit out on our daughter. What the fuck is wrong with you?" Lee yelled back.

"We don't even know if you *are* Rachel's daddy, Lee, so don't try poking your chest out motherfucker. Why the fuck you think, I was letting somebody else in while you were out working hard for me? I never gave a fuck about you, and the only reason it lasted as long is because your gullible ass never questioned Rachel's paternity," Debra expressed with malicious intent.

Rachel was listening to her parents go back and forth and started crying. She couldn't believe they still had this much animosity towards one another. Her mom was calling him "Daddy Maybe." Which only worked to piss him off further and before long they were screaming and hollering at one another completely ignoring the fact that she was even there. She had to try and end this cluster fuck. "You guys, hey…you guys…Mom-Dad." But neither of her parents heard her until she raised her volume to match theirs. "SHUT UP BOTH OF YOU, I'VE HEARD ENOUGH."

At her scream, both parties went silent.

Lee stared at her as tears streamed rapidly down her face. "I'm so sorry, Chelly," he said standing up and walking to embrace her to calm her down.

"Fuck that shit. Rachel you call me back when his punk ass leaves and don't try to avoid me cause if I have to come there it will be a problem," Debra finished.

"I'm sorry, but I can't deal with this please go," she suggested backing out of his hug.

CHAPTER FIVE

Around eight o'clock that night, Rachel was still processing the blowup between her parents along with the information that her dad had shared. She was barely holding onto her emotions and decided to call Dashawn. She needed her man, "Hello-hello, I need you baby," she sobbed out when he picked up.

"Are you ok? What's going on, Love?" Dashawn asked.

"Can you come over? I need you, baby," she cried.

"Uh, can you give me an hour to two hours, Love? I'm so sorry I've got to finish this presentation for work as it's due to my boss tonight."

"I understand, that's fine," she somberly replied.

"I'll be there as soon as I can love."

Rachel hung up and sat immobile wondering how her life could take so many twists and turns. Finding out that her mother had initiated the separation made her wonder how she could be bitter once her father decided to leave. And why she had to be the recipient of said anger, after all, she never asked to be born. Then, her phone sounded with her mother's ringtone. "Oh God, what now?" she questioned before picking up.

Before she could say anything, her mother started yelling, "It would have been nice to know BEFORE you put me on speaker that your sorry ass so-called Daddy was over your house, girl. I felt like I had been ambushed and you set me up for it. I don't know what I ever did to deserve such an ungrateful, no good daughter like you. You will never amount to anything. This is another reason why I wish I would have successfully aborted your ass," with that, Debra hung up.

Rachel's tears were flowing, and her nose was dripping. Her mother never allowed her to respond to any of her words and every one of them were released with hatred and malice. She sunk deeper into the couch unable to move or stop replaying everything that had been said by both parents as well as her mother now. "Why me, God? Why me?" she asked as she stared up at the ceiling.

Dashawn tried getting back to the presentation he was working on, but his thoughts were on Rachel. The brokenness that came through the phone was calling out to him in a way that made him force himself to focus. "Come on man, you've got to finish this presentation then you can get to your woman," he coached himself as he forced his mind to shift back to the task in front of him. As he typed quickly, he wondered what had set off this latest roller coaster it seemed as if the occurrences were becoming more and more frequent. *Her damn mother is trying to send me to jail.*

Dashawn was in love with Rachel and had told her as much. At the time, she was recovering from a nightmare and probably hadn't even realized he said the three words. Hell, he was shocked that he had expressed them at that moment, but he wouldn't take them back.

He would work to ensure that she felt his love in word and deed because the monster that was her mother was breathing everything but love into her spirit.

Two hours later, Dashawn pulled into Rachel's driveway and exited the car looking at the darkness coming from the house. He felt concerned, and he prepared himself as he knocked on the door.

It seemed as if Rachel was standing at the door waiting for him as she rushed to him putting her face into his chest with tears running down her face.

"What happened? What's going on? Baby?" he tried saying, but Rachel cried harder. "Alright, let's move out of the door." And instead of Rachel backing out of his arms, she jumped up and wrapped her legs around his waist. "Shit," he said as he attempted to close the door with Rachel tightly holding onto him. Walking carefully into the living room he gently sat on the couch, "So you want to tell me what's going on?" *Deep breaths, man you can't afford to lose your shit just yet. Hear what's going on first.*

Peering up slightly from his chest she whispered, "Dashawn, my mother has been trying to dim my light since I was nine years old. But recently she has escalated her behavior and treatment towards me…" she stopped as the tears began to fall faster. "I—I…" she sobbed unable to say anything else.

"Ok. I got you, and we can discuss this at another time. How about I run you a bubble bath and hold you until you can calm down enough to rest?"

"Will you get in with me?" She looked at him with red-stained eyes.

Dashawn gazed at her knowing that whatever she asked him for he would give her. "Your every need is my gift, Love. I'll be back in a second." He made his way to the bathroom. *God, how merciful will you be if I black out when I see her mom?*

Around one thirty in the morning, Rachel's phone started blaring and trying not to wake her, Dashawn slowly moved her out of his arms to grab it from the nightstand. "Hello," he answered. Hearing another man's voice on the line caused him to pause for a second, but he quickly learned that it was Kayla's husband Myles on the phone. "Man, I'm sorry I just got her to calm down and go to sleep. She called me over a few hours ago and had been crying since I got here. Why are you up and calling her this late anyway, man?

"I know it's late, and I'm sorry to bother you, but my Sweet Pea won't go to sleep," Myles grumbled into the phone. "And it seems as if her Auntie-God mommy is the only one who can calm her down and get her to sleep peacefully when we can't. I'm not happy about the call either."

"What do you mean she's been crying since you got there? Dashawn, what's going on? Sorry, you're on speaker phone," Kayla popped in from the background.

"Look, all I know is that something went down between her and her mom. Don't worry I'm not going anywhere. I'll be here all night I think I'll even stay with her tomorrow which is a good thing that it's Saturday because she's in no condition to go to work," Dashawn finished with a slightly agitated and raised voice.

"Don't worry about Sweet Pea, Dashawn we'll manage," Kayla concluded. "Thank you for coming over and taking care of her. I'm going to call some reinforcements to come over because we need to deal with this situation. It's been going on for too long, and now it's affecting Rachel more than ever. Have her call me when she wakes up please." She ended the call.

Dashawn walked into the bathroom to relieve himself, and since the door wasn't closed, he could hear Rachel talking in her sleep.

"Mommy, why can't I see him? I promise I'll be a good girl if you let me see my Daddy. But, he is, he is my Daddy. Oh God, oh God—please. God, why me, why me?" Rachel sobbed.

"What the fuck?" Dashawn shouted walking towards the bed. He grabbed her up securing her against his chest. "Come on baby, wake up it's just another dream."

But this dream must have been holding her in the contours of her mind because she wasn't waking up. Instead, she cried more and let out a few more things. "No, Daddy does love me. He told me he does. MOMMY, stopppppp. Please, don't hit me again. I'mmm sorry!" She cried out.

Damn it. Dashawn had never seen her this far gone. She had a couple of nightmares before, but this one was epic. "RACHEL, RACHEL, WAKE UP, WAKE UP. COME BACK TO ME. IT'S JUST A DREAM. RACHEL!" Dashawn yelled while shaking her.

Coming to, Rachel hugged Dashawn and cried. "Baby, it was so real," she told him.

"I don't know what happened in your past Rachel, but you have got to deal with it. I'm here for you. You need to let it out because with each nightmare the memories are getting worse. It's not healthy to keep things bottled up and trust me the hidden things don't stay hidden for too long." He kissed her forehead while hugging her to him in an embrace that was meant to strengthen her.

Rachel peeked up at him with tears lining her eyes and exhaled then she proceeded to tell him about the dream she'd just had.

As Rachel calmed down and fell back to sleep, Dashawn laid there with her in his arms pissed the hell off. *This bullshit is ridiculous. If I encounter that fucking bitch, there's going to be hell to pay.* He knew that he needed to rest to be available for Rachel but at this moment, he wanted to wrap his hands around her mother's neck and squeeze until she felt the level of pain that she was causing his woman. He laid on the bed with Rachel wrapped tight around him as if she would need the Jaws of Life to remove her body from his. "Rest Love, I've got you," he whispered in her ear.

It took him about an hour to calm himself down and sleep.

CHAPTER SIX

Around eleven thirty the next morning, Dashawn and Rachel were lounging in bed when her doorbell sounded incessantly. "Who the hell is going crazy on that damn doorbell? Stay here Love, I'll get it," he said getting up and slipping on a t-shirt and pajama pants. Stalking to the door, he was aggravated because whoever was on the other side wasn't letting up. "Hold the fuck on," he grumbled. Snatching the door open, he came face to face with a woman who looked to be in her mid-fifties.

She stared back at him with a clenched jaw and pinched expression as she tried moving past him to enter the house. "Who are you and why are you answering my daughter's door? Where is she any damn way?" she fired off.

God, is this a test? After everything that I've heard up to now, I know this bitch isn't trying to get froggy! "Excuse me, what?" Dashawn growled realizing that this was the woman that was causing Rachel so much aggravation. He disliked her immediately and could care less how she felt about him.

"Who the hell do you think you are? This is my daughter's fucking house, and I'm pretty sure you're just the latest piece of ass that she's entertaining. But talking to me with that tone will cause your ass to be gone in a second motherfucker!" Debra said snapping her fingers for emphasis.

"Who I am, is the man that will defend Rachel at every cost with no motherfucking hesitation. Name's Dashawn, you might want to acquaint yourself with it cause I'm going to be around longer than the second you just indicated!" He stalked off towards the bedroom. *She got me fucked all the way up.*

Rachel had heard the commotion and was moving around her room quickly putting clothes on when Dashawn entered a couple of minutes later. "So, I'm guessing my Mom is here, and you two have not only met but had some words as well, huh?" she asked.

"I'm sorry, but that woman is toxic as fuck Rachel, she entered this house like she owned this motherfucker. But why the fuck am I apologizing, she's the one with the problem!" he yelled out.

"Calm down, Dashawn. I'm not mad at you for exchanging words with my mother it just fuels her is all. I need to prepare for battle because between the explosion with her and my dad yesterday and your words just now, she's going to be livid," she started blowing out air. As soon as Rachel entered the living room, she saw Debra pacing back and forth with fire coming from her nostrils. *Oh Lord, give me strength.* "Hi, Mommy," she said to disarm her.

"Don't you fucking *Hi Mommy* me, little girl. Do you know that man had the gall to open his mouth to me? Who the fuck does he think he is? You might want to get your piece of ass in check because I'm not above giving him the business. You are already on my shit list for how you allowed Lee's punk ass to take over our conversation," Debra ranted.

"Uh, Mom what brings you by? You have gone from one incident to the next, and I just can't keep up," Rachel inquired trying to ignore everything that was said.

"First of all, don't come for me unless I send for you with your dumb ass. Did you hear anything that I said? You are as worthless as the piece of shit you *assume* is your father!" Debra steamed.

Dashawn was in Rachel's room trying to let Rachel handle the visit from her mother alone, but the longer he stayed out of sight, the louder her mother became and the words coming out of her mouth towards her daughter caused him to storm into the living room.

He had hit his breaking point, and it was time this bitch learned that today was her last day berating his motherfucking woman. *Nah, it isn't going down like this, fuck being a silent observer.* Before Rachel could respond, Dashawn went off, "You need to get the fuck up out of here. Rachel doesn't have to stand here and listen to you berate her anymore. When you learn how to act like a damn mother, then you can come back. But right now, I refuse to listen to any more of the filth spewing from that open hole on your face. GET. THE. FUCK. OUT!" he hollered marching toward the door. *She bout to find out how well she'll land on her feet.*

"I know good, and damn well you aren't about to let this motherfucker talk to me like this and call his self-kicking me out of *your* damn house, Rachel?" Debra questioned as she pinned Rachel with a look that caused her eyes to bulge.

"YOU HEARD WHAT THE FUCK I SAID, NOW BE OUT THIS BITCH BEFORE I HAVE TO

REMOVE YOU FORCEFULLY OUT!" Dashawn boomed.

"Oh, so his dick must be so good that you forgot how the fuck you came to be in this world. I should beat your ass for allowing this man who I have just had the displeasure of meeting to talk to me this way. You aren't saying anything in response just like you didn't when Lee spoke his trash yesterday. Oh, I'm going to leave, but you can bank on this, I WILL be back, and we WILL have the conversation that is only going to be worse now," Debra threatened as she made her way towards the door.

"Maybe you didn't hear me before UNTIL YOU GET SOME DAMN ACT RIGHT YOU ARE BANNED FROM THIS HOUSE AND HER LIFE, FOR THAT MATTER. Make no mistake I will NOT allow you or anyone else to harm her. Get your shit together or don't if you choose, but she is no longer a resting place for your level of fucked up bullshit!" *She's lucky my momma trained me not to hit women, fucking cunt.*

"Whatever, motherfucker. This shit is FAR from over. Rachel Spencer you haven't seen the last of me!" Debra yelled towards Rachel with ice in every word she spoke as she left the house.

Rachel stood in stunned amazement that Dashawn was kicking her mother out. His face was a hard mask, and his jaw was so tight that she could see a slight grimace from the pain he was inflicting on himself. "You do know that you have made this shit storm worse right? You do remember that she's my mother and won't go away that easily, right?"

"You know what, I'm not going to sit here and apologize for doing something for you that should have been done for you long before now. That woman is toxic, and I refuse to stand by and watch her belittle you, so that I can remember that she's your mother. Fuck that, she came up in here with the intention of destroying more of you than she already has, and I'll be damned if I allow it to happen on my watch. You can be mad all you want I was protecting you from her vile and demeaning actions. I make no apologies for it," he concluded.

Rachel smiled at him and walked over in front of him giving him a look of pure love as she leaned up and kissed him. "Ok then, go ahead and get your caveman on then boo. Now that we've handled that, what are we gonna do today?" she asked in an attempt to lighten the fireworks that just took place in her living room.

Dashawn took a minute to try and calm down it had been a long time since he'd reacted so aggressively, but that woman was lucky he didn't toss her out of the house himself. He wasn't the type of man prone to violence and definitely wasn't one to hit a woman, but that gotdamn woman almost had him forgetting himself. Taking a deep breath, he replied, "I know you're trying to shift the battle that just ensued in here but shit, I need a minute to calm down." He breathed in and out.

"The last thing I wanted is for you to have to react at all. I'm sorry that you had to meet my mother that way. If I could change the situation and your first impression, I would. I understand…" she stopped unable to meet his eyes.

Walking towards her, Dashawn spoke with each step, “You have absolutely nothing to apologize for. Nothing. So don’t feel sorry for anything that happened or was said. I’ve determined that you need a representative and I’ll happily accept the position. You never have to worry about anybody disrespecting you in my presence. That shit won’t work, and I don’t care who they are, if they can’t come correct when dealing with you, then they better be prepared to answer to me. Now, is there something you want to do with the rest of today?” he asked as he gave her a loving embrace.

CHAPTER SEVEN

Rachel had just finished recanting the recent events and blow-ups to Dr. Hawkins. "I think I fell in love with Dashawn after he expressed his protective dominance with my mother. Like I stood there stunned into silence, I mean I knew he was in this thing with me as he held me tight through the few nightmares I've had in his presence. But damn, the words he spoke to my mother gave me wet panties. I mean she was pissed about my silence, and I was standing there trying to control the slow drip from his words and protection. Awkward time to be turned on by your man, huh?" she finished smiling at the reminder of that day.

"So, with everything that happened, you only managed to hold onto how Dashawn defended you to your mother? That's an interesting concept and quite entertaining if I didn't have to try to analyze the meaning." Dr. Hawkins smirked.

"What's the point to be examined? I'm getting tired of crying and being depressed over the reckless actions of my mother. I think it's been long enough and I'm ready to move on. Tell me how to move on Sharon, because the rest of this shit is exhausting and unproductive in my life." Rachel sighed profoundly feeling exhausted.

"Are you ready to stop living in the past? Are you ready to deal with the things that have been said to you past AND present? How about are you ready to either establish a better relationship with your mother or remove her from your life completely? These are the questions that I'm posing to you today, Rachel. I need you to think long and hard about them and come to your next session prepared to answer each one. Whatever your answer is my job is to help you through it. That's our time for today." Dr. Hawkins stood up and walked Rachel to the door.

A few hours later, Rachel was sitting on her couch thinking about the questions Dr. Hawkins had asked her at the end of their session debating the answers. Picking up her phone, she dialed the conference call line that she and her friends had set up when they needed to speak in one sitting. "Hey everyone."

"Sister line, what's the crisis?" Jocelyn spoke into the phone first.

"Hello, ladies, what's going on?" Caressa inquired.

"Ok, so Maisha isn't happy that I shoved her into her daddy's arms with this sudden interruption," Kayla teased.

"I was in the middle of-uh never mind, my hubby is growling at the phone though, what's the problem girls?" Reia laughed.

"Um, I know I'm new to this circle but what's the emergency call for on a sunny Saturday afternoon? It's too pretty to be having problems." Monica quizzed.

"Well, damn I was in the middle of getting some ass," Charlene breathily fussed. "What the fuck? Unlike Reia, I ain't got time to sugar coat this interruption. Mark was in mid-stroke, get to the point so I can get back to making mine with him."

Rachel and the rest of the ladies laughed at Charlene's response to the conference call. "Sorry to bother you all but it was easier for me to get you all at one time," Rachel informed the group. "So, this was the option that way all of you can chime in and express your thoughts while allowing me to say this once."

"Ok, so tell us what's going on cousin," Charlene stated.

Rachel took a minute to gather her thoughts and then she said the two words that would begin the dialog, "My Mom." Before she could say anything else, the group began spewing varying comments as well as threats. "Ladies, as much as I want to hear all of your comments, I need you all to stop talking for a second and listen. Once I'm done filling you in, I will gladly listen to you all, but individually."

Ten minutes later, Rachel had conveyed the events that occurred within the last two weeks that none of her circle knew.

They all had expressed their thoughts on the situation as well as their views on what she should do.

Charlene's advice and comments held the most relevance due to their bloodline. "I say this from a place of unconditional love and understanding, but I think it's time for you to close this chapter of your life Rachel. You have been holding onto the fairytale concept of a mother-daughter relationship and truth be told it's just that – a fairytale. Aunt Debra is not interested in doing anything but destroying everything about you. Dashawn was right to speak up for you that day because you were never given an option to do it for yourself. I think you hold her to this high esteem and allow her to walk over you for the sake of saying that you have your mother in your life. But my question is, at what cost? It's time to move on. I also think that before you move on you need to have a conversation with Aunt Debra, so she knows that you're done. Leave nothing to chance and its time you spoke up for yourself. It's time that you told her how you feel and then move the HELL on with your life. You deserve to be happy, and I love that you have a man in your corner that is crazy about you. He seems to love you and want to make sure that nobody hurts you. I love it. It's time to get your very own happily ever after and this is the first step towards making that happen," Charlene concluded as the rest of the group co-signed.

At first, Rachel was emotional as she listened to every word her cousin spoke but the more she thought about it she couldn't help but agree with what she was saying. "As much as I hate to admit it, I agree that this is by far the most dysfunctional relationship in my life and it's exhausting as well as draining. But how will I get my mother to agree to such a conversation?"

"Why don't you see if your therapist can come over to your house for a Saturday session?" Monica suggested. "Then you can casually invite your mom to your house under the guise of wanting to apologize for your rude and disrespectful behavior."

"Uh, Monica I know you're trying to help and all," Caressa said. "But you haven't met Rachel's mom. That woman is batshit crazy. Sorry, Rachel and Charlene but the truth should be told without hesitation."

"Girl, please," Reia chimed in. "There's absolutely nothing to apologize for. We all know that woman is crazy, and this could be another disaster in the making."

Laughter was heard across the line as Jocelyn made another suggestion, "How about we plan to come out within the next two weeks that way we can be there for moral support or an ass whooping support or tag team?"

"I like the idea of having you all come," Rachel informed the group. "But I don't think the ass whooping will be necessary. Is it even possible for you all to come? I don't want to pull you away from anything for me, and my foolishness."

After they all agreed to be able to come out in two weeks, the topic moved on to something more enjoyable.

"So, once we get this shit done with Auntie Crazy, when is the next girl's trip?" Charlene forced out with a serious but slightly humorous tone. "I refuse to be excluded again. None of you all are secretly pregnant or trying to get pregnant right? Where are we going? Let's get something on the calendar now."

"How about we discuss that after we deal with Ms. Debra in two weeks?" Reia suggested. After all of that heaviness, we'll need a lighter conversation to delve into."

"Ok, that sounds good. Let me call Dr. Hawkins to set things up on her end. Then I'll call my mom and convince her to come. Oh, and shit, I need to make sure

Dashawn is here as well because he wouldn't have it any other way," Rachel finished.

"Yeah, you'll need him," Charlene concluded. "And his, uh-package afterward but he'll have to wait until we're done with our woman business. Shit with everyone in town, we might need to go paint the town red."

"Ok, I can be ready," Monica stated. "But I need one of you to show me a few fighting pointers in case I need to jump in."

Rachel laughed. "Girl, didn't you hear me? There won't be a fight!"

"Whatever, Aunt D. is gonna bring the heat," Charlene chimed in. "And we might have to subdue her ass up in there. Make sure you move all of your breakable shit."

The following Saturday, Rachel decided to discuss her past in detail with Dashawn as well as tell him that the meeting with her mother for next Saturday was set. With the help of Dr. Hawkins, she had called her mother to set up the meeting, at first, her mother was hesitant until she informed her that she wanted to apologize in person and she had a gift for her that would show her appreciation. With that done, she called Dashawn from her car, "Hi babe, uh how are you?" she hesitated.

"Is something wrong, what's that I hear in your voice Rachel?" he inquired.

"I'm ready Dashawn," she told him.

"You're ready for what baby? I'm not following you. Can you be more specific? What is it you're ready for?"

"Can you come over today? I'd like to talk to you about my past," she said in a low voice.

"Oh, when would you like for me to come over?" he asked.

"I'm home now, so if you're free, you can come over now while I have the nerve and withal for the heavy conversation."

"No problem Love. Do you need anything before I come? Have you eaten today?" he questioned.

"I'm good and yes, I had a little something to eat. I don't have much of an appetite right now," she whispered in a low voice.

"Alright, I'm on my way, but I want you to know that regardless of what you tell me it won't change my mind about you. I'm here for the long haul and if all others walk away, I'll be here and in your corner. I want you to remember that, see you in a few," he stated before ending the call.

CHAPTER EIGHT

Thirty minutes later, Dashawn sat next to Rachel on the couch feeling as if he could commit murder. He had gotten to her house about fifteen minutes ago, and at first, he just hugged her sensing that this conversation would be one that would shift them to another level of their relationship. He held her, providing the necessary strength from his body so she would know he was with her regardless. They had just sat down, and he met her eyes silently giving her an 'Anytime you're ready' look. What he wasn't prepared for was the words that would come out of her mouth—it upended all other thoughts swirling in his mind.

"My mother tried to kill me when I was ten, Dashawn. As a ten-year-old child, I couldn't imagine the level of hatred that could go into attempting such a thing. Oh, and it was the second time she'd tried. She recently informed me that she also tried to force a self-induced abortion while pregnant by throwing herself down a couple flights of stairs, but all she managed to do was kill the twin she didn't know she'd been pregnant with. My dad had no idea she'd been pregnant with twins and when he got to the hospital after the incident was only told that the baby was fine. Anyway, when I was ten, she nearly choked me to death because I wouldn't move fast enough when she asked me to. My only saving grace at that time was my cousin, Charlene's mom, Mae who stopped the attack when she walked into the house I had been visiting. I felt my life begin to slip from me and I kept thinking that I hadn't lived enough yet. I was ten fucking years old, and that was a thought running through my mind. Ugh. I remember praying that death would come and I kept asking God why I had to continue to suffer at the hands of my mother. My prayers began the year before when she became verbally abusive after her and my Dad split up. Shit, I came to realize that praying was my method of escape."

He sat there filling with rage and shock as he waited for her to finish.

"After my aunt thwarted her attempt, I began having thoughts of killing myself as her words grew more hateful and on top of that she began to abuse me physically. Extension cords, hair brushes, hangers, shoes, if she could reach it, she would use it. Do you know what it's like to feel as if no part of you was worth the body you existed in? I felt so isolated because my mother forced us to separate from her family after my aunt stopped her attempt. I wondered for years why my family even allowed me to return to her house after that. But she left that day and came back a week later full of apology, tears, and bullshit, and they all believed that she was remorseful, and I would be okay. Then she moved us without providing a forwarding address or phone number, so they were oblivious to the abuse that I continued to suffer." Rachel stopped for a minute to swipe at her tears.

He didn't know what to say. He felt too much anger to speak. He wanted her to get it out, tell him finally, what had happened to her as a child. So he fought showing his true rage or any questions he had, hoping she would continue.

"At thirteen, I ran away and ended up in a foster home where I stayed until I was eighteen as my mother refused to comply with the court rules to have me return to her care. Now, she's shifted to extreme verbal abuse now that I'm an adult. I'm not sure why I attempted to restore our relationship after I became an adult but when I turned twenty-five, I got the bright idea that I needed her. Now eight years later, I'm starting to wish I would've left that dumb ass idea alone. When she found out that my dad and I restored our relationship which was against her wishes, she intensified her hateful treatment."

Dashawn watched Rachel fight back the tears that were welling up in her eyes, and it made him violently angry, yet he had to keep it together for the sake of allowing her to release her pain. *Fuck the consequences... that woman needs a dose of her own medicine.* "So, what makes you continue this farce of a relationship now? I've witnessed her abuse firsthand, and when she has no regard for other people witnessing her attacks, that's a real problem," he asked moving her over to straddle his lap.

"I'm tired now baby. Tired of hearing her shit, tired of taking her abuse, I'm fucking tired of it all. I deserve more than she's ever given me and now, I understand that I don't have to take it. I'm ready to be happy," she said as she breathed in and out slowly.

"You're damn right you deserve more, and as the man in your life, your happiness is something that I'm here to ensure. Next week, we'll be ready and as a united front, this shit will end," he said wiping tears away with his fingers. *For every tear this beautiful being sheds, her mother should receive a blow to her gotdamn face.*

"Yes, it will. Next week, I'm going to end our relationship. For me to move forward, I've got to release myself from this dysfunction. It has caused me way too many headaches and shit heartaches for that matter. Thank you, Dashawn."

"You never have to thank me, Love. I'll stay over with you Friday night and whatever you need from me, I'll provide it for you. Now, is there anything else that I need to know?"

"I love you, Dashawn Sanders. You are heaven sent. I'm amazed by the love you show me because after everything that I've endured, I didn't think that somebody would have the ability to love me past all of my pain." She leaned into his chest, hiding the tears that she could no longer prevent from falling.

"One thing you never have to question is the love that I have for you, and it honors me to hear you reciprocate my feelings," he stated as he brought her face out of his chest and gave her a tender kiss.

His emotions were taking a nosedive as his mind whirled with everything she had informed him of. *My fucking heart is bleeding.* Like her, he couldn't believe that her mother could be so hateful and so reckless with the life that she created. He was pissed. He'd be at the meeting ready for her shit and capable of tossing her ass on her face if need be. It was time to move forward and without the bane of her mother's existence. He was ready and up for this challenge, because something in him was telling him that this meeting wouldn't be without an explosion of sorts. *This will end next week, and we can move on with our lives.*

Later that evening, Rachel was contemplating the conversation with Dashawn as she remembered how tight his lips were, his jaw was tight, and although she was sure he was unaware, his fists were balled. He had a look of death on his face and she knew that if her mother were anywhere in the room at that time, he would have snapped. *If just that brief recant got him that upset what will next week be like? Hmm, guess I'll find out then.* "It's Saturday night and this is our usual date night what do you want to do?" she asked him but before he could answer her phone rang displaying her father's number. "Uh, hi Dad. How are you?"

"Hi Chelly, I'm uh-uh, I'm not doing too well at the moment," Lee replied in a troubled voice.

"What's wrong Dad?" she asked as she sat upright on the couch as she took note of Dashawn scooting closer to her.

"I'm sitting here and feeling like shit, Chelly. I know that I missed a good portion of your life and all of your childhood. All I can say is that I'm sorry. I'm sorry for the pain my absence created. I'm sorry for the abuse you suffered at your mother's hands as well as the verbal abuse she doled out. Mostly, I'm sorry for failing you. My prayer is that you will find it in your heart to forgive me. I can't go back to any of the past, but I can make sure that I secure a better future. I want to establish a relationship with you that is lasting and forever from this point on. Will you please grant me access to any aspect of your life?" he concluded sniffling.

The words her father spoke left her feeling as if she'd been pushed over, she'd wanted to have a better relationship with her father, but her mother stood in the way as she tried to appease her. But it seemed as if now that she was about to end that tumultuous relationship it would be replaced by another parent who could fill a small void. It took her a long moment to get herself together before she could respond, "Uh Dad—um—I—uh," she stuttered still having difficulty gathering an adequate response.

"I know this seems out of the blue Chelly, but I've been thinking about it ever since that explosion between your mother and I a couple of weeks ago. I realize that part of her abuse is my fault and I should have never allowed her to dictate my actions completely. I should have fought harder for you and my part in this mess. I'm so sorry," Lee finished exhaling deep.

Rachel was trying to wipe the tears making a fast track down her face but when they wouldn't slow, she gave up. As she looked beside her, she was met by Dashawn's puzzled face and mouthed, *I'm okay babe.* "Alright, uh-Dad, I accept your apologies, and I genuinely appreciate it. I've been waiting a long time to embrace a relationship with you. I'll let you back in wholly on the condition of you showing the effort. I can't put myself out there to have my heart broken, and I would like to know that if the relationship is progressing it's happening because you genuinely want it to happen."

"I understand that completely, how about I take you to dinner this evening as a first attempt at moving forward. Contrary to what I've shown, I love you with all of my heart Chelly."

"Well, let me check with my boyfriend about dinner he's here and Saturdays are when we usually have a date night. Hold on a sec, Dad," she said.

Before she could mute the phone, her dad spoke again. "Why don't you bring him along Chelly, I'd love to meet him," Lee offered not wanting to let the opportunity slip through his fingers.

"Ok, let me talk to Dashawn, and I'll send you a text with a time and place. How does that sound?"

"Sounds good Chelly. I'll be waiting to hear back from you." With that, he hung up.

CHAPTER NINE

The Friday before the sit-down meeting with her mom Rachel sat in her kitchen staring at her coffee mug wondering how the meeting would go. She had hopes that things would go well, but she felt apprehensive. Her mom could be hostile and she wasn't sure how it would go with so many people in one room. But regardless of the outcome, this meeting would proceed, she just hoped that it would be amicable. As she raised her mug, her doorbell sounded alerting her of an unexpected guest. When she reached the front door and peeked out, she smiled big as she saw her circle of friends on her front porch. "Well, I'll be damned. I can't believe that you all showed up and why the hell are you dressed in army fatigues and timberlands? Monica? You too? What are y'all preparing for, crazy asses?" She laughed as she widened the door letting everyone in.

"Shit, you thought we were playing!" Charlene stated. "We ready for this shit storm, and if Aunt D come up in here with her bullshit, we will be whooping some ass up in this bitch." She walked toward the living room with the rest of the troop following behind her laughing.

"First of all, the meeting is tomorrow afternoon," Rachel said looking at Jocelyn with a pitiful look. "And secondly, I told y'all that no ass whooping would be necessary. What is wrong with you all? Jocelyn, you're usually more level-headed talk these nutjobs down would you?"

"As much as I like to be the level-headed sister and all that shit," Jocelyn deadpanned. "I've had enough of this bullshit and seeing you hurt. So I've come prepared to open up a can of whoop-ass myself!"

"Fuck that! Caressa ranted, "If Debra's ass comes up in here saying anything other than she's sorry and a sorry excuse for a gotdamn mother than I'm going to kick her arse myself!"

"We've been watching you suffer for years, and her ass needs to learn not to fuck with you from tomorrow forward," Reia concluded.

"Come on you guys, and y'all even dragged Monica into this?" Rachel laughed. "Look at her, like she knows anything about cans of whoop ass." She stared at Monica in her getup.

Monica snickered. "Girl, I know more than you think, and I might be new to this group, but I'm anything but new to fighting. I can bring it too, besides who do you think suggested the matching outfits?"

At this, all Rachel could do was laugh along with the rest of the group thinking that her circle of support would make tomorrow's meeting interesting. She loved them for showing up to support her and fight on her behalf if the need arose. "Alright, crazy women of the suburbs, what y'all want to do today? I should be heading to work but seeing as how my boss is standing here playing hooky, I guess I'll call my assistant and do the same," she stated looking at a smirking Kayla.

"I thought that we could go find a *bye bitch* gift," Charlene suggested.

Looking around at the women gathered in her living room, Rachel was caught off guard. "Uh Char, what the hell is a *bye bitch* gift?" she questioned with raised eyebrows.

"It's a gift that you'd give Aunt D to show your relationship has ended after you tell her *bye bitch,*" she concluded as she shrugged and began laughing hysterically as the other women joined in.

"You are a damn fool and did you forget that this *bitch* is your aunt?" Rachel shook her head.

"Right. Charlene, don't you feel a little bad for being in this circle with us and ready to fight your own aunt?" Monica asked shaking her head.

"You know what? Hell no, I don't feel bad," Charlene stated angrily. "My aunt is a psycho, and I've seen the effects of her abuse on this beautiful woman we all love standing in front of us. I'm sick of it! Aunt or not, this shit is wrong, and I'm on the side of right. Fuck the bullshit if she attempts to lay a hand on my favorite cousin, I'm going to intervene!"

"Uh, I appreciate you all coming," Rachel expressed with a serious tone. "But I'm saying again, it won't come down to intervention or fighting. I'm going to handle this meeting and put my feelings on the table amicably. It's going to be just fine."

"You know that sounds really good," Kayla said cracking her knuckles. "But let's be rational here and prepare for fireworks and mayhem."

"OK, I think our sister has forgotten who we're dealing with. Who brought the Vaseline?" Reia asked.

Rachel just shook her head and laughed as the women went back and forth over their plan to be ready for tomorrow. She silently thanked God for their friendship, sisterhood, support, and love, as she would never be able to get through tomorrow's encounter without them. She also hoped things wouldn't come to the nightmare they were anticipating. "Alright, I think since we're all together, we need to hit up *Club Flight*. I'm pretty sure you married chicks haven't been to a club since y'all got tied down and shit. Did any of you bring any nightclub attire?" She smirked looking around the room.

"I live in the city and am not aware of this *Club Flight*," Kayla probed. "You're in a relationship, so how do YOU know about it, Rachel?"

"Where is Dashawn that you are even allowed to go to a club?" Charlene taunted. "His sexy ass is gonna let you go out tonight?"

"Honey, the last time we were together and went to a club, I recall Dashawn snatching your ass up and carrying you out of the club," Reia joked. "Oh, and shit, Kayla's ass ended up the same way. I'm not sure that we really need to be in a club after the way you two experience that type of setting."

"Baby, the way Dashawn's milk chocolate melted into Rachel's ass that night," Jocelyn teased. "I thought we would be seeing more than her white dress on the dance floor!"

"First of all, I can go wherever I damn well please," Rachel stated firmly. "I'm a grown ass woman, and I make my own decisions. I—" she stopped as her phone went off. "Damn, y'all talked his ass up!" She strode out of the room to answer Dashawn's call as they all laughed.

Dashawn arrived at Rachel's house around twelve-thirty Saturday morning as she was returning from hanging with her sister-friends and cousin at Club Flight. Part of him wanted to express his displeasure with her going to a club with men pushing up on her as he had a mental recap of how she could potentially dress. The other part of him said to trust that she would be decently dressed with their relationship status in her mind. As he met her in her driveway, he determined that maybe he should have set some guidelines. "So, uh, did you really wear that shit to the club tonight Rachel?" he quizzed taking in her wardrobe choice.

Just then, her group waved and laughed as Kayla backed out of the driveway.

Rachel was wearing some royal blue off-shoulder dress that stopped above her knees and appeared to be see through. While she looked amazing in it, he was aggravated that she wore it outside of his presence. Fucking her right here would probably be frowned upon.

Looking down at herself she shrugged. "I'm covered up this time Dashawn, what's the big deal?"

"You're barely covered up, is that damn dress see-through?" he grunted.

"Can we take this in the house? You're… uh-raising your voice and we're outside. It's late and I'm tired we have a big day tomorrow," she spoke hesitantly.

"Yeah, let's go in the house and talk about this shit. Did you forget that you're not available anymore? I don't appreciate your attire and again, is that damn dress see-through?" he grilled walking to the front door inspecting the dress closely.

"Listen, I think you're overreacting Dashawn. My dress is lace with a slip type material underneath. It is also just slightly above my knees, so please calm down babe. Also, the girls and I were just hanging out. I stayed in the booth because we were too busy drinking and enjoying each other's company to get on the dance floor. You don't have to defend our relationship status or puff out your chest because I was an honorable girlfriend tonight," she stated on a tired exhale.

He'd gotten a look at the dress and determined that she was fully covered underneath making him realize that he might have overreacted a little bit. "I'm sorry Love. When you told me you were going out, I had a memory of our first encounter and I momentarily got territorial. I'm sorry, let's clean up and head to bed. We need to sleep a little before the meeting."

"I understand how you and I met but let me tell you that after that encounter, I have been off the market ever since. Insecurity is unnecessary as you are who I want, okay?" she provided as she grabbed him around his waist.

"Ok…." With that, he hugged her and walked to her bedroom. "Let me show you how secure I am."

Later that morning, Rachel was lying in bed with a faraway look and tight smile causing Dashawn to probe, "What's that look on your face Love?"

Rachel was running through the many scenarios that could play out with the meeting, and she was saddened by what she would have to do. She knew it was necessary, but it didn't make the decision or outcome less difficult. "I was just thinking about one of my fondest memories of my mother a few years before I was placed in foster care. She used to have a garden and would spend a lot of time tending to it. She also had quite a green thumb and grew her own roses. One morning, I got up and was searching for her when I heard her voice in the backyard. She was singing to her flowers and the look on her face was one I've rarely seen from her. I remember standing in the door in awe of how happy yet content she was as she sung to those rosebuds. Eventually, she looked up and noticed me standing there, she waved me to her then held my face in her hands as she continued singing to me in such a loving manner. I don't know how today will go, but I will always remember and cherish that memory," she concluded wiping the tears that had fallen from her eyes.

Hugging and caressing her from behind he spoke, "I know that it feels as if you're never going to recover from this moment, but I want you to know that it will get better. My wish is that your mother will come to realize that you mean more to her than the hatred she's feeling and selfishly holding against you. Try not to worry about what's going to happen. I've got you," he whispered.

Rachel was stuck in her head as she could only nod her head it was comforting to know that he was here with her and would be with her throughout the entire meeting. She needed his strength and as he held her, she knew that she would be okay regardless of what happened in the meeting. But right now, she needed a distraction from her mind. "So how's work going? I've been so preoccupied that I forgot to ask you about the presentation you had not long ago. Did it go well, babe? Catch me up."

"Are you sure you want to talk about my work right now?" he asked.

"Of course, I do. Besides, I need a temporary distraction," she told him as she snuggled into him preparing to listen to his update on his work life for the next thirty minutes. This conversation was normal and relaxed. She would learn that the one to be had in a few hours would be anything but ordinary or comfortable.

It would turn out to be the shit storm everybody, but she…had predicted.

CHAPTER TEN

Twenty minutes after two, Rachel fidgeted on the loveseat in her living room wondering if her mother would even show up. Everybody but her mom had arrived and the quiet chatter was making her antsy. “Did you all remember to park down the street from my house? I don’t want her realizing she’s walking into an ambush,” she stated clasping her hands together then abruptly standing and walking to look out of the window.

Needing to try to calm her down Dr. Hawkins announced to the group, “Yes, we all parked away from the house, so it’s very inconspicuous. Try not to worry, Rachel. Why don’t you try calling her to see if she remembered?”

“Oh—I hadn’t thought about t-that,” she stammered out and grabbed her phone dialing her mom’s number. “Hi Mom, I was just wondering if you were heading to my house?”

She had barely got this out before her mother was snapping her response back so loud everybody in the room heard her, “I’m on my fucking way I’ll be there in ten minutes damn!” her mother shouted and disconnected the call.

“Lord, give me strength,” Caressa grumbled.

“Jesus be a wheelbarrow, cause this bitch about to get rolled out this motherfucker today,” Dashawn snarled as he walked over, kissed Rachel tenderly on the lips and hugged her to him caressing her back.

"Well, shit we might not have to go too heavy on the Vaseline girls," Jocelyn said cracking her knuckles. "It looks like Dashawn didn't come to play with Mommy Dearest,"

Rachel turned to look out the window again and saw her mother pulling up. "Shit, she's here. Go to the kitchen everyone. I need to ease into this shitstorm subtly and please be quiet," she pleaded as she ushered them all quickly into the kitchen. "I'll be fine," she said to a hesitant and slow-moving Dashawn.

Walking towards the door, Rachel said a quick prayer as the doorbell began ringing incessantly. *God, it's me, please give me the strength to do what I need to do.* "Hi Mom," she greeted as she opened the door allowing her mother entrance.

"It took you long enough. Shit, you just called me why weren't you standing by the fucking door?" Debra ranted stomping in the house then into the living room.

Rachel took a slow breath before silently expelling it from her lungs. *God, are you listening?* "Uh, sorry."

"Yeah, you are and wasting my time so get to the point. I don't have all afternoon to waste on the likes of you."

"Ok, I brought my therapist here to help me apologize in the right manner. Let me get her, she's uh—in the kitchen," she quickly finished.

"I know you didn't bring me here for no bullshit," Debra flung the words hatefully.

"No bullshit, she's just helping me and I wanted her help in formulating a proper apology. Be right back." Her strides were hurried to escape a comeback from her mother. As she entered the kitchen, she was met by angry faces. "Why are you all looking like you been sucking on lemons or some shit?"

"Don't do that shit Rachel!" Charlene spoke in an enraged tone. "We heard every word Aunt D let rip and if you didn't walk in here when you did, we were walking out of here to snatch a knot up in her ass."

"You got that shit right," Dashawn agreed. "And I bet I don't stay up in here another minute while she thinks you're taking her shit. So yeah, let's go. I'll sit in the corner and try to keep my mouth shut for now, but that will depend on her, and her bullshit." He marched toward the door.

"How about we all going out there cause I'm ready to set it off up in here," Caressa added.

Before anyone else could utter a word, Dr. Hawkins chimed in, "Everyone, can we please try and calm down? Cooler heads have to prevail here. My job today is to make sure we stay on course to reach Rachel's goal."

"That all sounds good and all Doc, but that bitch better bring her shit under submission right quick, cause we ain't come here to play with her today," Reia stated as she tied her Timberlands tighter.

"Alright, listen can you come in the room after fifteen minutes?" Rachel requested. "She might lose her shit once Dashawn enters with Dr. Sharon. If you all come too, she will lose it, and there is something I must say to her first. Oh, and I have to present her with her gifts," she added nonchalantly.

"Gifts? Rachel have you lost your ever-loving mind?" Jocelyn whisper-yelled.

"Trust me I haven't," she said as she motioned for Dr. Hawkins and Dashawn to follow her back into the living room.

Dashawn was trying to hold onto his tiny thread of patience as he entered the living room.

But no…Rachel's mother was slowly cutting it with every word out of her mouth.

"So, I guess your stupid ass forgot to mention that this punk ass dick of yours was also in the kitchen huh?"

"Oh mom, I thought I mentioned that he would be here. I'm sorry. Anyway, can we take a seat, so we can continue?" Rachel attempted ignoring the insults thrown.

"You might want to sit by him because I might slap the shit out of you, depending on how this continues."

"I guarantee you won't be slapping a motherfucking thing, least of all my woman," Dashawn shot back. "Keep talking and your little ass will be the one slapped."

"Motherfucker, please! You aren't invited into this conversation. I'm not even sure what the fuck you're doing here."

Before Dashawn could respond, Dr. Hawkins cut in, "Can we not lose sight of why we're here? Rachel asked me to come here to help her apologize and release some things to you. Rachel, the floor is yours."

"Bitch, who are you?" Debra inquired.

"She's my therapist, Rachel attempted to explain. "Dr. Sharon Hawkins, Mom. Let's continue shall we?"

Dashawn sat down next to Rachel on the couch as she sat directly across from her mother. His temper was flaring and he was fighting the rage that was threatening to overtake him. *1.2.3.4, keep counting cause if you snap right here, somebody will lose their life.*

Rachel took the floor just as her friends and cousin silently crept into the room. Her mother was so busy glaring at Dashawn that she hadn't noticed their entrance.

Rachel shushed them with her hand. "Uh, mom, I called you over here to get some things off of my chest but first, I want to present you with a gift," she stated as she handed her a gift bag.

Debra's eyes lit up as she snatched the gift bag and removed the contents of what was inside. She smiled broadly when she pulled out a silver bracelet and noticed the rhinestones surrounding the word "MOM." But her excitement turned to anger once she pulled out a plaque reading the words engraved on it. Down the left side was "MOM" with the following inscription in the center:

You have SHATTERED ME with your words.

BELITTLED ME with your venom and ENTANGLED ME with your rejection.

I PRAY that God has mercy on you.

Until you change,

Rachel

"BITCH. Did you? What the FUCK?" Debra yelled out as she threw the plaque down and proceeded to stomp on it.

"From the age of nine, I have been tormented and tortured by you and as of this minute, I'm releasing you and your fucked-up version of motherhood from my life. You no longer have control over my life, my emotions, nor my happiness. Cherish these gifts because they're the last you'll ever receive from me. Oh, you forgot to read the other side of your bracelet. In case you refuse to look now, it says, "***WORLD'S WORST EXAMPLE***" because you certainly suck at being a mother. Now you are at this moment released from duty. GET. THE. FUCK. OUT. OF. MY. HOUSE," Rachel stated fiercely in a dismissive tone.

Instead of leaving, her mother lunged towards her, but she was shifted out of reach by a quick moving Dashawn.

Her circle of friends and cousin stepped in front of her as a human barricade.

Charlene clenched her fists. "Aunt D, I suggest you get out of here while the getting is good."

"Fuck you and that little bitch behind you. I'm about to kill her motherfucking ass in here tonight. She forgot who brought her into this world and I'm gonna remind her as I take her out of it!" Debra yelled as she attempted to get around the women.

"I can guarantee you that the only way you're gonna get to her is if you get through all of us, Jocelyn seethed with an authoritative tone. "Now, we're trying to show a smidgen of the respect you don't deserve. So I suggest you get your ass out of here before we help you out of here."

Rachel stood off to the side blocked by Dashawn and her human barricade feeling mentally saddened by everything that her life was up to this point. As tears began streaming from her eyes, she fought to keep the overwhelming sense of loss from coming out in front of everyone. It seemed as if a rabid dog bit her mother and she continued trying to go around the people blocking her.

Before Rachel lost it altogether, Dr. Hawkins walked over and began whispering so only she could hear, "I know that you feel as if this decision isn't the right one but take comfort in knowing that you're doing what's best for you. One day, you're going to look back and wonder why you didn't make the decision sooner. So, head up young person, there is a better life on the other side of this separation. Is there anything else that I can do for you today? It appears that you have an iron-clad support system for the rest of today's transition, so I feel comfortable leaving you in their capable hands," she said as she noted Dashawn's unmovable stance.

"N-no, I-I think I'll be okay. I'll call you to schedule my next appointment," she whispered back.

"Alright, well let me get out of here, so I don't have to admit to being visible when the ass whooping takes place because it looks like your mother is ready for a fight." Dr. Hawkins smirked as she gave Rachel a one arm hug and walked rapidly to the front door.

"I'm guessing that a fight is what you're itching for," Reia ground out. "But I promise that you won't be laying a fingernail on Rachel."

"What you bitches fail to realize is that I will get to this bastard kid one way or another." Debra glared at them all. "So, we can stand in this position and stance all motherfucking day, makes me no never mind. I'm beating her ass today, and if any of you want to join the beat down then I have some hands for you too!" She continued trying to get around them.

"FUCK THIS SHIT! GET HER ASS OUT OF HERE BEFORE I GET HER THE FUCK OUT HERE!" Dashawn yelled.

Before anybody could grab Debra, she swung and punched Charlene in the face then proceeded to keep swinging. "Since you want to be her protector, I'll beat your ass instead!" she ranted as she swung.

From the first punch, Charlene reacted as her mom and Charlene exchanged blows.

Rachel noted the enraged and blank look in Charlene's eyes and knew that she reacted to the hit and could care less about her fighting her mother's sister.

"You lost your gotdamn mind putting your hands on me Bitch!" Charlene yelled.

"Oh my God, somebody stop this shit before it escalates further?" Rachel hollered.

"Bitch, it's escalating anyway!" Debra screamed as she charged Rachel and managed to get a hit off in her face.

After that, the scene became chaotic as Rachel walked around Dashawn and the others as she and her mother started fighting. Before she could get too caught up in it, Dashawn grabbed her and moved her out of the way again. "No Love, you are already dealing with regret. I won't let this be one more thing for you to chastise yourself about later."

Debra was unrestrained, so she started swinging at the other women, and before long they all began swinging back.

All Rachel could do was watch the scene in front of her as she watched her best friends and cousin take turns exchanging blows with her mother. If it weren't so severe, it would be comical as they acted like they were in a boxing ring. It was a one on one fight and when one got tired, they would walk out of the line of punches to allow somebody else to get a turn.

"Have you had enough of this bullshit today? It ends here, so I suggest you stop fighting and leave now!" Charlene informed Debra.

"Make me leave!" Debra raged back.

Damn, did this bitch take some drugs before she came over? Rachel watched her mother still full of energy and hatred. She was in awe at how she seemed to be holding her own in the multiple fights.

At the moment, everyone was stopped in a defensive stance with heaving chests.

"Mom, can you please just leave? I'm done and so is this farce of a relationship," Rachel sighed out.

"Y-y-y…" Debra attempted to speak, then grabbed her arm and reached for her chest. "I-I c-can't. My c-chest," she stuttered as she hit the floor.

"Son of a Bitch! Call 911, this ignorant disgrace won't die here!" Charlene yelled.

"Well, I guess we found a way to make her leave," Caressa stated with a small smirk on her face.

CHAPTER ELEVEN

Dashawn sat next to Rachel in the waiting room at the hospital unsure of how he should feel. He could care less what the outcome was but based on how she responded he knew that Rachel wasn't immune to her mother or her wellbeing. As he rubbed her back, he felt the mounting tension radiating through her. "How are you holding up Love?" he inquired.

"This day has been one clusterfuck after the other and I never expected that this would be the outcome when I set up the discussion. I-uh, I'm not sure what I should do here. Like, a few hours ago, I kicked her out of my life, and now I'm sitting in the ER waiting to see what's going on with her as she collapsed in the damn living room. Oh, and this occurred only AFTER she attempted to kick everybody's ass in the room but yours. I don't know what or how to feel right now Dashawn," she finished tiredly.

"I can't tell you how or what to feel right now. However, you're entitled to feel however you want," he told her. *But she deserved this shit.*

Before she could reply, Charlene, Caressa, Monica, Reia, Kayla, and Jocelyn walked into the waiting area with unreadable expressions on their faces.

"Where have you all been and what's with the looks on your faces?" Rachel quizzed.

Shaking her downturned head, Monica spoke for the group, "I think we're all just wondering how Crazy D went from fighting all of us to this moment we're in right now. It's weird how it went down and the mystery of all mysteries"

"Uh, Crazy D?" Rachel asked laughing.

"Hell yeah, did you see her little ass taking on all of us?" Reia stated with a puzzled look. "She's like four feet something, for goodness sake. Shit, only a crazy person would engage in a fight with six different women at the same damn time. I mean who does that?"

"OK, we assumed she was fucking crazy before, but now I think she's certifiable," Caressa added. "Had us all trying to catch our breaths in between punches and her little ass was bouncing around like she was swatting flies. Bullshit!"

"Had me feeling like I was on Monday Night Raw or whatever that damn wrestling thing is. Shit, I'm gonna have to hit the gym after today." Jocelyn nodded. "I didn't know I had to be in shape to keep up with Coo-Coo D. This is some straight up bullshit."

Dashawn looked at Rachel, and they started laughing hysterically which caused the rest of the group to start laughing as well. He was feeling a little better seeing Rachel smiling even though the situation was far from humorous.

At that moment, the ER doctor came in with a bewildered look on his face. "Uh, Rachel Carpenter?"

"It's actually Rachel Spencer, but that's me. How's my mother, doctor?" she asked pointing to her chest.

"Touch and go, to be honest, your mother suffered a massive heart attack and we almost lost her. She's gonna need surgery and they're prepping her as we speak, would you like to see her before we take her?"

Rachel stood there stunned unbelieving that her mother had a massive heart attack that would lead to surgery. "Oh my God," she said staggering a little bit as Dashawn stood behind her wrapping his arm around her waist. "Yeah-uh yeah, I-I want to see h-her," she stuttered.

"No problem, but you'll have to go in alone," the doctor informed her. "We want to keep her calm beforehand, and since you're the only next of kin, you'll be the only person permitted in the pre-surgical area."

"Alright, doctor. I'll be back everyone. Can you all wait for me?" she asked with a whimpering tone.

"Nobody's going anywhere Love. No need to ask, see you in a few," Dashawn stated giving her a quick kiss before the doctor escorted her out of the waiting area.

Dashawn silently watched Rachel follow the doctor and his nerves escalated as he hoped that the wicked witch of motherhood would be on her best rational behavior. He couldn't expect her to have a good behavior personality after what she had shown so far. It was so rare for him to see a mother such as Rachel's, as his mother was the most loving and sweetest person he knew. Not everyone was meant to birth children and they should have removed her ability when she hit puberty. *Then my love wouldn't have had to suffer.* As he stewed in his thoughts, he heard the ramblings of her friends and cousin.

"So Charlene, have you called any of your family about your aunt's illness? What about your mother?" Monica questioned with raised brows.

"I called my mom on my way here and I'm supposed to keep her posted. So I suppose I should do that now. Aunt Debra isn't very receptive to the family including my mother as she isolates herself from all of us."

"Why? Is she not receptive other than the fact that she's batshit crazy?" Reia asked.

"Girl, that's mostly it. She and my mom fell out years ago for something she did to Rachel, so that covers her. As far as the rest of the family, uh, she's never been close to anyone. Then they all know she's fucking nuts." Charlene shrugged.

"We all know she's insane but how come nobody in your family defended Rachel?" Again, Reia questioned. "We've been around since third grade and the transformation from then to now, has been intense. I'm sure as her cousin, you've had lots of angry moments about her treatment but how will your mom and family handle you and her fighting?"

"Well, it's a long story and this isn't the time to go into it really. I also shared that with my mom and she wasn't happy about the encounter, but she also understands that I was protecting and defending Rachel. Rachel and I have always been close, so when she hurts, I hurt and she's been holding this mess in for a long time," Charlene stated releasing a subtle breath.

Dashawn sat listening to the conversation and it still puzzled him how Rachel fought this fight with her mother alone for so long. It was almost like she was on a crazy solo island where it was just her and her mother with no rescue in sight. Entering the conversation he stated, “Despite what has happened in the past… from this point on, she’ll never have to walk through this or anything else alone again.”

“Dashawn, please be patient with her. You’ve witnessed the things that her mom is capable of, so this hasn’t been easy for her,” Caressa said wiping tears from her eyes.

“Don’t worry, I’m more than able to handle her issues, and I’m here. I love her and one day, she’ll be my wife, so this is a part of the journey toward the rest of our life together. No worries ladies, I’ve got her,” he stated looking each of the women in the eyes, so they could see how serious he was.

“Awww, that makes me happy. Thank you for loving her the way that you do. You’ve been exactly what she’s needed,” Jocelyn said softly as the others nodded in agreement.

“No thanks needed ladies. Now, let’s get off all this heavy talk. I want to treat my Love to one of your girl trips. After all of this, I think she’ll need an escape sooner as opposed to later so, where can you take her?” Dashawn asked peering around the room.

Rachel walked into the pre-surgery room to see her mother’s eyes closed. “Mom?”

At first, she thought her mother was sleeping, but her eyes opened and darkened into a hateful sneer.

"Why are you here bastard child? I thought you told me to exit stage left? I haven't forgotten your dismissal and I'm not sure why you feel like you should be here. I'm done with your ass, you caused this heart attack, and I'll never forgive you for taking me away from my plans for tonight," Debra told her raising her voice with each offensive word she spoke.

Gasping, Rachel gaped at her mother as if she had two heads. "Are you serious right now? You are moments away from going into open heart surgery and you still can't be civilized and act like my fucking mother? Wow!" She backed away from the bed.

"Fuck you and your faux sympathy, Rachel Spencer. I'm not interested in you or anything else about your existence. The moments and incidents at your house sealed our fate, laying here made me realize that my wish of having you gone was granted, so thank you. I'm finally rid of you. I just wish I didn't have to have the stretch marks reminder. Now get your bitch ass out of here and don't come back!" Debra spat closing her eyes dismissively.

As Rachel walked out of the pre-surgery area, she was numb and jilted by her mother's reaction. *Even in extreme illness, this woman couldn't humble herself, my God.* Needing a diversion to gather her wits before going back to the waiting room, she headed to the hospital chapel. A few minutes upon entering, she was consumed with emotion and dropped into the back pew. Bowing her head slightly, she began praying knowing that she needed help.

God, it's me, Rachel. I know it's been a while and you're probably not happy about what you witnessed earlier today. But God, you know I've been holding all this sh—stuff in for a long time, and it was only a matter of time before it came out. Even though I can't handle my mom in my life anymore with how she currently is, I'm asking that you cover her in surgery. I don't want to have today's event be the same day she leaves this world. Now, I don't care that she might die one day, I just don't want my conscience beating me up that it was the same day that she fought me, Charlene, and the girls. So, if you could grant me this mercy request? I'd appreciate it. Thank you, God.

Rachel walked back into the waiting area with a lighter step and a smile on her face. She knew that it would take a while for her to return to normal emotionally, but when she left the chapel, she left those issues sitting there. It was time to move on and as she looked at the people she loved, she decided that the time was right now. "Y'all look like you're up to no good." She smiled.

"Ok, so it looks like you're just coming back from slipping yo momma a secret pill," Jocelyn inquired. "What's got you smiling like a damn Cheshire cat?"

"Nope, but THAT was my final goodbye. She cursed me out and kicked me out. I'm free, who's hungry?"

"Um, cuz, you sure you're good?" Charlene asked as she looked at Rachel strangely. "Did you check yourself into the crazy ward while back there?"

Dashawn stood up and walked toward her with an intense look as if he was searching her soul. “You good, Love?”

“Truthfully, I’m not sure if I’m good now, but I will be. Thanks for being here babe. Now really, who’s hungry? I’m starving,” she said rubbing her stomach.

“You never have to thank me, Love. I told you, I got you.” He leaned down and kissed her.

“Well, if all is right in Rachel’s world, I could eat.” Reia smirked. “I think we all worked up quite an appetite messing around dabbling in fight club 101, like we were trying out for a marathon or something!”

“Cool, let’s get out of here. What are we in the mood for?” Rachel asked as they headed toward the exit. “Oh shit, let me give them my number just in case,” she said before rushing to the nurse’s desk to leave her contact information.

“Well, some things take longer than others.” Jocelyn smiled.

The others shook their heads at Rachel while Dashawn grunted.

CHAPTER TWELVE

A month later, Rachel was going through security at the airport, excited about the much needed, much-anticipated *Girl's Trip* as the last vacation that they'd taken when she had met Dashawn and Kayla met her husband, Myles. They were all long overdue and needed this trip to solidify their sisterhood and connection. This time, they were adding Monica and her cousin Charlene to the mix, so it should make for an exciting but fun adventure. They decided to keep it simple, so they were heading to Vegas to paint the town red for a few days. Since Kayla was still relatively a newlywed and new mom, the trip was only four days, but they could do a lot in four days. As she looked at her travel partners, Kayla, Charlene, and Monica, her grin widened at the debauchery that would go down. "Ok, listen I don't know about the rest of you, but it's about to go all the way down in Sin City," she promised.

"Hmmph, there's only so much you can do since you're someone's girlfriend Rachel but yeah ok." Kayla smirked.

"Right, I'm a girlfriend, not a wife, so that means I'm still a free agent," Rachel boasted.

"The HELL you are, Dashawn's ass made it quite clear that you are attached and unavailable to anything other than meal intake. I don't have time to argue with somebody else's man ESPECIALLY when I sexed my man so good last night that he'll forget I'm even out of the city until I return," Charlene bragged as she did a quick little shimmy.

"Well since I'm not dating anyone, I'm free to search with hopes of locking down my forever like you two did on the last trip." Monica lifted her brows towards Kayla and Rachel.

"Oh honey, no, no, no. Sin City is strictly for sin, booty calls, sightseeing, shows, and gambling," Charlene informed a confused looking Monica. "The only things you'll catch that'll be forever are certain types of STDs. You're going to the wrong place for permanent!"

"Come on now, those are all stereotypes, and I don't think that they're accurate at all," Monica replied stoically.

"Well, your brother made it clear that I would bring you back the same way you left." Kayla shook her head. "And we won't even mention your dad's comments."

Monica laughed. "Girl, my daddy only made those threats for Myles' sake. Trust me, he would love for someone to take me off his hands. I'm still in his pocket. So yeah, I doubt he was that serious!"

"Fine, but I'm not interested in finding out one way or another," Kayla huffed.

"Alright you Debbie Downer…" Rachel walked towards the gangway. "I'm not interested in this shit. I want to explore as much fun as these four days will allow. Now, come on they're calling our group!"

Meanwhile, Dashawn was sitting on his mother's couch discussing Rachel. "So, do you think I should hold off on asking her to be my wife? I mean she is fresh off the mess with her mom. I so wish you could have been in that living room to mop her up with the floor. The way she treated and talked to Rachel was anything but motherly. I had to remember that you raised me to be respectful towards women, cause I wanted to snatch her little ass up and toss her out of that house."

"Son, I'm glad that you remembered your manners and my teaching…" she paused laughing at his facial expression. "No, really it's a reward worthy cause I'm sure you wanted to break out your superhero cape, but had you done that you might have lost the woman who's seemed to have stolen your heart. As far as popping the question, what do you feel you should do? Personally, I love Rachel for you. For some, she may be too flawed but remember that even diamonds start off scratched before they shine brightly," his mother concluded.

Dashawn sat there for a minute searching his heart for the answer to his mother's question. His search made him travel back to when he knew he wanted Rachel forever it was the morning after the explosive meeting with her mother.

He was lying in bed holding Rachel as she released the tears that she'd probably been carrying for her entire life.

...He felt every drop that hit his chest, and it caused his own chest to break and his heart to tighten. As he held her, and the sobs became more pronounced, he felt every emotion she couldn't communicate. He knew that he would hold her as long as she needed as well as be there to rebuild and restore her in every way. He merely laid there knowing that after today, she would be ready to move forward with her life. His emotions were going haywire, as he couldn't understand how her mother could knowingly spew so much hate, but he learned that her mother had no kindness or love to give or show her only child.

After minutes that felt like hours passed, he leaned down and whispered in her ear, "Today is the last time that you will ever feel like this so release everything so that you can move forward. I'll be here to wipe away all your tears. I'll be here to ease your fears. To mend your broken heart... to love away your pain. I'll be here to comfort and restore you, to cherish you. I'll be here forever. Let it go, Love. I've got you," then he hugged her tighter, as her sobs racked her body...

"I knew a month ago that I wanted forever with that woman and now it's time to make things official. For Rachel, actions speak louder than words, as she's been hurt, and sight is better than speak. You just prepare for a new daughter and I'll let you know once the engagement is official." He smiled.

"Well, I'll be damned! My son is gonna make some woman an honest woman. I get to have a daughter finally. Let's do this baby, I'm ready. Then you can get busy making me some grandbabies." His mother smirked.

"Slick, adding that little bit in there, but don't worry you'll get what you want in due time. I do want to say that I'm honored to have such a loving and supportive mother such as you. One thing this experience with Rachel has shown me is that I'm humbled by the love you have for me as well as our relationship. Thank you for always being my Rockstar. I know it hasn't been easy, but you've done a hell of a job Ma. I appreciate you more than words could ever express. I gotta run." He hugged and kissed her then headed out the door.

"Do you see this shit?" Reia pointed laughing.

"Yup, and I want to know if he really lives up to it, gives you an authentic interpretation of dickhead doesn't it?" Charlene joked.

"Well, how about we ask him to give us a peak?" Rachel teased.

"We haven't been here twenty-four hours yet and we already run into some foolishness." Jocelyn shook her head.

"I want to know why he thought walking around in a penis costume was the thing to do and are his balls really dragging the ground." Caressa examined the guy strolling in front of them.

"Hmmph, doesn't look like we have to wait l-long," Monica sputtered. "Will you look at this mess? He's taking off the—costume!"

"Oh, my-damnnnn!" the girls spoke simultaneously.

The man in front of them had taken off the costume and underneath he only wore boxer briefs with very sculpted abs and a sizable boner.

"I guess you shouldn't judge a book by its cover, under that penis was a very impressive looking dick, or so it appears," Charlene alleged.

The man began walking toward them with a snide look on his face.

As he got closer, they wondered just what he was about to do.

He stood in front of Rachel and adjusted himself suggestively. "How about I show you just what lies beneath, and then you can decide for yourself which one you like the most," he mocked.

The women began snickering at Rachel's expense as they watched the emotions playing across her face.

"She said she wanted this time to be loaded with fun!" Kayla giggled.

"Baby, while I'm sure you are working with something impressive." Charlene snickered. "I'm not sure that everybody on this strip is willing to find out just how impressive it is. Besides, I'm not too keen on letting the world see what's mine expressly. Now if you want to offer a private viewing, we can work something out."

"I bet I could show you enough to wet your dreams and make your pussy cream," the man said still adjusting himself.

"Come on," Jocelyn muttered. "We have things to experience and being annoyed by this man is holding up our adventure. Let's keep moving, trust me we'll see a lot of creepy things along the way."

"I agree, he might be packing more than an impressive dick behind those shorts and hell… he could be a walking virus for all we know!" Caressa declared unmoved by the man's imprint.

High fiving Caressa, Rachel stepped out of the man's path. "Right, I'm ready for a drink. Let's move."

Dashawn laid in bed holding his cell phone to his ear listening to Rachel recount her initial 'welcome to Vegas' greeter. "So, were you actually going to take him up on his preview offer? I mean if a preview is what you're looking for, we can switch this call to video, and I'll give you a view worth seeing Love…" His voice dropped huskily.

"I might take you up on that offer later, but for now, keep it warm for me baby," Rachel teased.

"Whenever you're ready, I'll be ready. Remember this though, if any previews will be given or cocks viewed it will be mine and mine alone. You're mine, and you should know that I'll castrate whatever dick attempts to come towards you and my treasure," he promised.

"Ooh, baby talk dirty to me because you know I enjoy when you get all territorial," she replied seductively. "No worries, you're imprinted in all the right places,"

"Believe me I'm not worried. I trust you explicitly don't forget it was my idea for you to make the trip. Now get off this phone and rest up. I'm sure you will be in for quite a time over the next three days. Enjoy yourself and I'll see you when you get back. Love you," he told her as he prepared to hang up.

"Alright Baby, I was just teasing you. I'm happy to hear that you trust me. Now, I'll see you when I get home. Do you want to meet me at the airport or my house?"

"I'll do you one better. I'll pick you up from the airport and take you home. That way, I answer both requests at the same damn time. Goodnight Rachel."

"Oh yeah, I definitely like that idea. Goodnight Dashawn and I love you too."

Dashawn hung up the phone and contemplated how he would welcome Rachel back home properly. He knew she needed this break. He just hoped it would give her another opportunity to unwind.

CHAPTER THIRTEEN

"So, who's been practicing their Kegel exercises?" Charlene inquired. "I think since most of you are married, you don't need to as you should be well worked out, but I hear this class will push you."

Raising her hand— "I'm not married, but I'm well versed in Kegel 101,"—Monica said winking.

"Oh, you are a freak, huh?" Charlene laughed loudly.

"Shit, I'm not married and it's been a while since I've used certain muscles," Rachel interjected despondently.

"Uh, what do you mean by that?" Reia asked. "And why the heck are you looking like somebody kicked your puppy?"

"I've been too stressed out to have much sex." Rachel dropped her head.

Caressa spoke while looking confused, "Uh, first off, what? Secondly, what?"

"I'm still stuck on why we need to do Kegel exercises." Jocelyn glanced around the group.

"So, for us baby making married women it helps with urinary incontinence which can happen after childbirth," Kayla added, educating the group. "For you single folks, the area of importance is cutting down a man's premature ejaculation. Although, I sure ain't got time for quick spurts either."

“Uh huh, Rachel you over here with desert cunt,” Charlene went back to Rachel’s comment shocked by the news.

“Desert cunt for real Char?” Rachel shook her head. “It’s not deserted. It’s just been on hiatus for a while. I’m surprised Dashawn hasn’t pushed the issue or mentioned it.”

Monica chimed in, “Maybe his main concern has been on making sure you’re good after all of the crazy you’ve had lately. Maybe he too, hasn’t realized it’d been a while.”

Reia laughed. “So, what the hell, did we come on vacation with Dr. Phil’s kid? Girl, lighten up on the miseducation from Mimi.”

At this comment, all the women including Monica giggled. They were waiting for their stripper class to get underway. It was one of the last things on their to-do list before they headed home. They all wanted to learn some new moves to demonstrate on their men. Thankfully, it looked as if they would have the instructor to themselves which would be perfect.

“Afternoon ladies, how’s it going?” the petite but toned instructor greeted as she walked over and shook hands with each one of them.

Charlene walked around the pole closely inspecting it. “Baby, it’ll be going very well if you can teach me how to get my ass on this here pole without going home with a broken ankle, vagina or anything else I might need to use on my boo.”

“I know that’s right, girl!” Kayla snickered.

The instructor looked excited for this. “Oh, I can see you ladies are about to be one of my best classes. Okay then, everyone grab a pole. I want us to start off slow and work up to other things. This is Stripper 101. So no sense in jumping in, as if you have experience.”

“I actually have experience and have taken several of these courses before,” Monica bragged.

“Well, damn your ass withholds information,” Reia interjected. “Why are we paying for this class when freaky Monica could have taught us all of her tricks?”

“Ok, ladies. Let’s get started, first off, my name is Cinnamon, and after we finish this course, you’re going to also come up with a name that will go on your certificate of completion. So, think about it now and in the meantime, let’s get moving. For the next hour this piece of steel is going to be a simulation of your man.” Cinnamon smirked as she walked over to the radio to start the music.

Dashawn stood in front of the jewelry counter and contemplated the rings that were on display before him. He’d been standing there for just under ten minutes trying to decide on the best ring for Rachel. “Damn, give me a minute, I need to call back up,” he told the sales clerk grabbing his phone to call Kayla. But her phone went straight to voicemail, so he decided to call his mother. After all, she was a woman and would know what would be acceptable. “Hey Gorgeous, how are you today?" He smiled into the phone when his mother picked up.

"I'm well baby. How are you, is everything okay? I sense a little something in your voice."

"How do you manage always to know when something's off with me, Ma?"

"I spent twenty hours of labor and thirty-six years with you that's how. Now, what's going on?" she interrogated.

"Alright, I'm standing at the jewelry store, and I've been trying to pick out the right engagement ring for Rachel. I want the perfect ring that's both something she'll love as well as a perfect representation of her. I just thought I could pick your brain, so you could help me decide," he concluded.

"You want to tell me how I can help without seeing the choices? Switch to FaceTime, I need to have a visual to help."

Quickly switching to FaceTime and turning the camera to the rings on the counter, he asked, "So what do you think about these, any of them seem like Rachel from your interpretation?"

"Hmmm, give me a minute to look son."

"I remember how nervous she was to meet you and she didn't know that I too, was anxious." He laughed at the memory when he introduced Rachel to his mother, just over eight months into their relationship…

... "You have nothing to worry about Rachel, my mother isn't one of those mothers," Dashawn said rubbing her hand as he drove to his mom's house.

"So, you say but what if she doesn't like me or think I'm good enough or maybe she has someone else in mind for you? That sort of thing happens all the time Dashawn." She worried her bottom lip.

"Well, if she doesn't like you I'll disown her," he teased.

"You will not but thank you for trying to lighten the situation." She smiled.

"Alright Love, we're here so take a deep breath," he coached her after parking in the driveway and exiting the car to come to open her door.

"I'm ready, I think? Uh, so how far is the bus stop in case I need to make a mad dash and need a place for Uber to pick me up..." She exhaled quickly while doing a quick glance around at her surroundings.

Dashawn laughed while escorting Rachel to the front door and squeezing her hand reassuringly. He knew she would be just fine.

A few minutes after ringing the doorbell his mother opened the door with a frown on her face.

Oh, shit wasn't expecting this, he thought as he spoke, "Hi, Mom. What's wrong?"

But his mother stood there with that same frown as she took in Rachel, then looked at him. She hadn't yet invited them into the house, and he was silently panicking thinking she was about to make him out to be a liar. He peeked at Rachel, and she stood rigid with a grimace marring her face as well.

A few seconds later, his mother started laughing as she dropped her arms and hugged Rachel. "Hi Sweetie, I'm sorry for teasing you just trying to have a little fun at your expense because you looked scared shitless when I opened the door. I'm Sandra Tate." She snickered.

Once he heard his mother's words, Dashawn breathed a sigh of relief.

"Hi Mrs. Tate, it's nice to meet you. You almost had me backing up and heading to the nearest address for an Uber pickup..." Rachel exhaled...

...."I thought I had scared her right out of your life. Her face looked so funny, I couldn't keep up the act." His mother laughed breaking into his walk down memory lane.

"All I kept thinking was she made me out to be a liar, and I'm really feeling this woman. That was a cruel joke Mom," he kidded. Now here he was asking her opinion on Rachel's engagement ring.

"Well, I've learned she is tougher than nails and it would have been an uphill climb, but you might have gotten her back."

"This woman has forced me uphill ever since we returned from that cruise. But it's been worth it, she compliments me. Now, which one do you think?" he quizzed steering the conversation back to the rings, as the saleswoman grew fidgety.

"I like that one in the middle," his mother said.

"That's the one I was thinking as well. Good choice, Ma."

"Damn, anybody else extra charged and wishing their man was here for a demonstration of what they learned?" Caressa asked.

"Nah, I think I worked some muscles that have been idle, and I need a good soak," Rachel quipped.

"Hmmph, I think this driver needs to get us back to the hotel faster, cause I'm about to go have some intense phone sex with my man. Caressa is right and I need a release really quick," Charlene informed them as everyone laughed.

"Uh, TMI. Some things don't need to be shared." Jocelyn shook her head.

"Oh, so Rachel and Caressa's subtlety was better? Y'all know that I'm not interested in beating around the bush," Charlene finished right before they pulled up at the hotel.

"Alright, I'm hitting a few machines, I'll check you out later ladies," Jocelyn said over her shoulder heading toward the slot machines.

"Wait for me, I want to try my luck," Reia yelled while running to catch her.

"I'm going to take a quick siesta call my room if you need me," Kayla informed the remaining women.

"A siesta for what, your old ass is too young for naps," Monica told her sister in law.

"Well, I've been napping with Mai and I have a schedule to keep if I expect her to keep hers," Kayla snapped walking away.

"Well, I'm about to change into my suit and relax these muscles in the hot tub," Rachel added.

"Now, that sounds like a good idea. I'll meet you there," Monica said.

Rachel entered her room feeling tired but aching enough that she rushed to change into her swimsuit instead of taking the nap she wanted to take. Needing to hear his voice, she decided to call Dashawn. "Hi honey, how are you? You miss me yet?"

"I missed you the minute you left my presence and I knew you'd be gone for days. How's Vegas treating you? I hope you're having a great time."

"Vegas has been wonderful and definitely treating me right. I wanted to hear your sexy voice before I raced off again, that's all."

"I'm glad. Although, you sound tired, make sure you're taking care of yourself out there. I don't want you coming home sick, cause you've run yourself ragged."

"No worries, I'll be just fine. I gotta run now babe, I'll see you soon," she wrapped up the call, giving him an air kiss.

"Uh huh, now you gotta run. Alright, see you soon Rachel," Dashawn joked and disconnected the call.

An hour later, he was still pondering his conversation with Rachel. She sounded tired causing him to worry about her. *The woman is going to come home sick, I better stock up on the essentials.* His thoughts were interrupted by his phone, "Yo man, why you only harass me when Shauna leaves you? Dang, you think I'm your backup or something? What gives?"

"Come on dawg, who said Shauna was even here today?" Ronnie snapped back. "I don't only call you then. Stop tripping. Do you want to hit up a club? I know your woman is out of town, so I'm sure she's living her best life, while your ass sits around moping around at home and shit. Come on dude, the first round is on me," he offered.

"Man, fuck you. Ain't nobody moping around. How you know I'm at home anyway, with yo punk ass?"

"Aw, here we go with the bullshit. You out in the streets already, where at? I'll meet you and buy the next round."

"I'm at the crib, but my point is… don't assume shit. Where you trying to go? I gotta work in the morning."

"A'ight, how about we hook up Friday and go to that new club ya woman and her girls went to?"

"Nope, man, Rachel will be flying home Friday night and I got to pick her up from the airport."

"Oh, and I guess you need to handle yo business with you trying to play all coy and cool. Yeah, I know you need to do more than pick her up from the airport she's been gone all week, huh?" Ronnie cracked up.

"Whatever. You just mad cause Shauna left your punk ass again and you trying to figure out how to fill the void. Don't be hating cause my woman actually enjoys spending time with me. Now since you in your feelings and shit, let me get off here and go grab something to eat cause I'm guessing we ain't going nowhere tonight." Dashawn laughed at Ronnie's expense.

CHAPTER FOURTEEN

"So, you can tell things have changed a little bit since we hit up a club," Kayla teased. "When we went on that cruise, we were living it up. Now, we're all covered up and dressed like respectful women."

"Yeah, it's very ironic that you all are pretending as if you were perfect angels on this damn trip when I heard how you left the Caribbean," Charlene vented. "I'm guessing we need to go on another cruise, so you Mother Theresa's can let it all hang out. Choosing to be undercover when I travel with y'all asses. I'm offended."

Monica nodded looking grumpy. "Say that. Rachel and Kayla's ass left a club upside down based on how they walked in it and now, we're walking up in HERE in pantsuits and shit. What gives?"

"Had either of you explored YouTube or Facebook for other footage of these shows you'd understand why we're rocking these pants," Caressa informed the complaining women.

"Let me enlighten you both." Jocelyn did a quick shimmy and continued walking to the line. "What you *don't* want to do is get flipped up in the damn air with a dress on and be ass out in a room full of other women. So yeah, I'll proudly strut my ass in this jumpsuit."

"Right, while I'm all for checking out the Magic Mike's premiered in this show." Reia shrugged. "I just don't want to become a part of the views that will be on display. No way, my husband will stumble upon my treasure from a leaked video, no thank you. This here jumpsuit is my treasure's security blanket."

So here, a day later, Rachel's time in Vegas was over, and she was sitting in the airport waiting to board the plane home. She'd been tired and feeling sluggish. Hopefully, she wasn't coming down with anything, but she'd been sneezing all day, her nose had been running, and her voice was extremely hoarse. She was feeling worse as the time ticked by. "Damn, I'm going to go home sick and have to hear Dashawn fuss me out or say he told me so."

"That's what happens when you think you can party like a Rockstar without keeping yourself hydrated in the process," Kayla told her.

"It was a good ride though." Rachel laughed remembering the events from the night before.

"Rachel, how are you gonna explain to Dashawn why you're so hoarse?" Monica curiously questioned.

"I'm not. He heard how tired I was a couple of days ago, so I'll just play into my getting sick. No big deal."

Charlene shook her head as she laughed. "So, the fact that you were dry humping not one but multiple guys in the show while shouting, *ride it daddy* isn't the cause? How about the fact that we nearly had to hunt down smelling salts to revive your ass when Channing Tatum came on stage at the end?"

"Ok, but in my defense, it was Channing-Mother-Fucking-Tatum! I would have had the same reaction had Dashawn been in the room. Of all weekends for his sexy ass to make an appearance, he chose the weekend when

I was in the audience and almost in the damn front row. Shit, I think my panties are wet just from the thought of it. That man is one of my celebrity crushes, and I make NO apology for my reaction," Rachel concluded with a roll of her eyes.

"Uh, that's all well and good but Rachel," Kayla stated. "Your ass screamed loudly and then dramatically fell onto the stage with a fake ass gasp and grabbing of your chest."

Monica nodded. "I know. I was worried that you were having some out of body experience or something or that you really needed medical attention."

"Oh, I needed some attention all right." Rachel fanned herself. "And I'm going to remember that and the entire show as soon as I get in front of my man. Whew!"

"You're a damn fool. Let's get on this plane so we can get home," Charlene finished heading to the gangway.

Dashawn stood at baggage claim waiting for Rachel to debark the plane and retrieve her bags. He was waiting with Kayla's husband Myles who was holding their daughter Maisha, and Charlene's beau Mark.

"So, when are we taking a guy trip, Shawn?" Myles cooed. "Our women take trips to continue their bonds. I think we should begin a ritual of our own."

"Man, right now I'm not sure if you were talking to Maisha or me. Why the hell are you cooing?" Dashawn asked while looking disgusted.

“Damn, my bad dude. It’s just been my Sweet Pea and me for four days and I forgot how to act around grown-ups!” Myles laughed.

“Ok, that right there says we need this posed guy trip expeditiously,” Dashawn scoffed. “Let’s call the other fellas and set something up. Here comes our women and fuck… Rachel ran herself down anyway!” He pointed toward the four women approaching them.

“I know what you’re thinking, and I feel fine,” Rachel squeaked out and then sneezed.

“Really, what am I thinking? I can almost guarantee that you aren’t close.” He pinned her with a look expressing his frustration. “I want to spank your stubborn ass. How long has this been going on?”

“Why are you yelling? I’m standing right in front of you. I’ve only been like this, uh-maybe this morning…” She looked down not meeting his eyes.

Dashawn stood there staring at her for a minute knowing that wasn’t the truth. He’d spoken with her a few times, and she’d been working overtime each time. “Yeah, alright. Let me get you home and to bed,” he told her as she sneezed again. *Damn, I had other welcome home plans for her.* “Uh, Kayla, if Ms. Fine *isn’t* in on Monday, she’ll be right in bed,” he informed Kayla over his shoulder.

“No problem, I don’t want her passing her cooties all around the office anyway,” Kayla responded after she kissed Myles and took Maisha out of his arms.

"I said I'm fine, so I'm not taking that nasty medicine, and you can't make me," Rachel whined to Dashawn two hours after she got home.

"You barely have a voice now, and you've been sneezing almost every five minutes. Take the damn medicine stubborn ass," Dashawn expressed unhappily holding the spoon of cough suppressant to her mouth.

"Humph," she grumbled as she quickly swallowed the horrible tasting medicine. "I want you to know that I had other plans for you picking me up tonight," she said before sneezing again.

"So, did I but you don't see me throwing that in your face or the fact that you weren't supposed to come home sick. Now lay down while I let my mother in with your soup." He kissed her and walked toward the door.

"I have no idea why you called your mother and dragged her out of the house this late for me anyway," she stated to his retreating back.

"Because I love you…" he called over his shoulder, "….and she loves you. Now just rest, will you? I'll be right back."

Rachel hadn't realized that she'd dozed off until she was woken up by a gentle kiss to her forehead. As she pried her eyes open, she noticed that it wasn't Dashawn kissing her. "Uh, hi Mrs. Tate. You didn't have to come all the way over here for me," she screeched out.

"Nonsense Sweetie, I'm happy to do it. How are you feeling? You're warm, has my son taken your temperature yet?" Mrs. Tate quipped looking toward Dashawn who was entering with a tray filled with stuff.

"I don't think so, but I'm not really sure, to be honest. You'll have to ask him, oh and can you get him for being an ogre too?" she whined.

"Sure, thing Rachel." Dashawn grinned. "Why don't you sit up and let me feed you some of this soup? It's my mother's homemade chicken noodle soup recipe, so it should taste good."

"Uh, Mrs. Tate you just have homemade chicken noodle soup lying around? I haven't been home long enough for you to whip up a batch and then drive all the way over here in two hours," she questioned.

"Oh, heavens no, sweet girl. Dashawn asked me to make a batch after you two talked last, he had a sneaky suspicion that you'd be sick when you returned. Now come on and eat a little for me." She laughed.

Rachel smiled as she sat up with Dashawn's assistance and took a small bite of the soup that was being offered to her. She loved how she felt surrounded by him and his mother. It had been a long time since she'd had a mothering hand in her life. *Hmm, I could get used to this.* "I appreciate you doing this for me, Mrs. Tate," she said before she started coughing followed up by several sneezes.

"It's my pleasure Rachel," she told her smiling widely.

Dashawn woke up Monday morning when he felt overheated and realized that it was Rachel snuggled under him as if he were her warm blanket. *Guess she's*

not going to work after all. Leaning down, he tried to check her temperature by how warm her forehead was subtly. When that trick failed, he eased her aside and got up from the bed to grab the thermometer. Re-entering the room and reaching the bed, he urged, "Wake up Love. I need to check your temperature." He lightly shook her.

"I'm not sick and don't have a temperature," she grumbled as she burrowed further into the covers.

"Humor me, woman. According to you, you're fine. But I've been playing nurse all damn weekend. Now open your mouth so I can check for a fever, stubborn ass." He smirked as he inserted the thermometer when she turned over. "Just as I suspected, not sick huh?" he asked as he showed her the stick that showed one hundred and two.

"Damn it, I can't miss work today!" She coughed into the covers.

"Oh, you're missing work and not leaving this bed or house today. I need to run out for a little bit to grab some things from my job. Is there something you need while I'm out?"

"No, I'm fine. Thank you…" she bellyached and pouted.

"Stop pouting. I'll be back soon, oh and stay in this bed," he told her as he kissed her forehead.

"Grrrrr…" she growled at him as he smirked and left her room.

A week later, Rachel was laying on the lounger in Dr. Hawkins office wondering how long she would keep up this cycle. “Sharon, would you be offended if I stopped coming here every week?”

“Are you feeling as if you’ve processed enough to warrant these visits being stopped or spaced out?” Dr. Hawkins inquired.

Thinking about that question a little further, Rachel continued to lay there but then she came up with her answer, “I wouldn’t have progressed this far without the ability to talk things out with a neutral party. My support system is phenomenal, but they are also protective of me, so I occasionally withhold my feelings from them.”

“So what feelings are you bottling up? I’m here to be your person to unload freely. What can I help you process through today, Rachel?”

Sighing deeply, Rachel decided just to let it go, “I know that I left my mother’s hospital room with the intention of leaving her life, but I can’t help but regret that decision a little bit. I mean I’m not glutton for punishment or harsh treatment. I just wish things were different is all. I’ve always held out hope that she would change, and we would have a normal mother-daughter relationship. It just saddens me is all,” she concluded.

“What you have to consider is how much sticking around would have cost you? You’ve been allowing yourself to be a doormat. I know… don’t look at me that way, but you’ve been laying down and being a doormat since you were nine. It’s time for you to stop giving people opportunities to destroy you. Your value is greater than you've been told in your past. Be okay with the separation dear. You deserve to be happy."

"But I want a relationship with her, why won't she just love me like I need to be loved by her?" she stopped as she broke down sobbing.

"That's a question that no one can answer but your mother, and right now she's unable to answer it either. I also must prepare you that you may never get the answer to that question as your relationship may never be reconciled. If that's the case, I want you to release yourself from the guilt of walking away. Remember that the pain that you feel and felt in the past caused you to want wholeness as opposed to brokenness."

"I'll try to remember that. Thank you for everything Sharon. I'll see you in two weeks instead of next week. I'm gonna see if I can stretch my visits to two weeks instead of one."

"No problem, but remember, I'm here should you need me sooner."

CHAPTER FIFTEEN

A month after Rachel and her crew came back from their girl's trip, Dashawn sat around a cigar bar having a good time with Myles, Justin, Carter, Brian, and his best friend, Ronnie. "Man, this has been just what I needed. I think our women are on to something with these trips. I could get used to this. How often y'all want to have a man-cation?" he paused from taking a drag of his stogie.

"You know you ain't bout this grown man life, stop fronting," Ronnie clowned him.

"Fuck you, don't start your bullshit tonight," he retorted while chuckling.

"Ronnie, how long you and Shawn been cool?" Brian questioned.

"Uh, me and this chump been boyz since we were in high school. We met when we played each other's basketball team for our neighborhood recreation centers. I thought this dude was some preppy punk until he schooled me on the court. He talked shit the whole time which made the loss my team took worse."

"Right, and I'm still schooling your ass on the court. You ain't learned shit in all the time we been friends. Your game is still weak and so is your three-point shot!" Dashawn laughed. Before they could continue going back and forth his phone buzzed with his mother's picture. "Hey Ma, how are you?"

"Son, uh where are you? His mother probed.

"I don't like the sound of your voice. What's wrong?"

"I don't want to worry you, where are you son?" she asked again.

"Ma, we're way past worry right now, what's going on?" he pushed.

"Baby, I'm not sure if it's possible, but you might want to try and get home as soon as you can."

"What are you not saying to me, Mama? Please stop going around in circles. Just tell me what's going on," he forcefully pressed.

"Uh-it's-uh, Rachel, son. She and I were having lunch and she got a call from the hospital. Her-uh-that woman died—she's, uh, Rachel isn't handling the news well. She needs you." She sighed.

"FUCK! I'm going to find a flight and get home as soon as I can. Are you able to stay with her until I get there?" he asked dejectedly.

"Of course, no need to ask. I'll see you soon," she told him before hanging up the phone.

Dashawn hung up and immediately called the airline to change his flight. *Of all times for me to be out of fucking town. Damn.* After changing his flight for later that night, he looked around the room at the men who were surrounding him with curious expressions on their faces.

"Is something wrong, man?" Jocelyn's husband, Justin asked.

"Man, of all mother-fucking times to be out the city. Rachel's sorry ass mother dies and I'm not there. She's falling apart and I need to get home," he grumbled.

"Damn, man. Is there anything we can do?" Reia's husband Carter spoke up.

"I don't even know right now. I'm just anxious to get to my woman. Let me get back with y'all once I know and have assessed her needs." He dapped each guy and headed out to get back to the hotel to grab his clothes so he could get to the airport. This shit was about to be crazy.

An hour before the hospital call…

Rachel was sitting across from Dashawn's mother enjoying her company. They'd been out shopping, so now they were having lunch. "Mrs. Tate, thank you for taking time out of your Saturday to spend with me." She grabbed and squeezed her hand.

"It's been worth every minute, and I have enjoyed it just as much as you have. Remember, I don't have any girls, so I love having you around to go shopping with me. Dashawn frowns if I stay in the stores too long. He's not into shopping. When he was younger, I used to drag him into all kinds of stores and then I'd force him to stand outside of the fitting room for hours while I tried on outfits." She giggled at the memory.

"Oh goodness, no wonder he doesn't offer to accompany me shopping. You've scarred my boo for life." Rachel hollered with laughter.

"Maybe a little but he got over it once he got to his pre-teen stage and became more observant of the women coming in and out of the changing rooms. After a while, I had to stop taking his eager ass with me." She smirked.

"Yeah, I bet he was watching more than clothes being taken into those rooms," she teased.

"For sure. So I'm excited to have someone to tag along with me again. Thank you for being a willing participant. I love spending time with you and hope we can do more of these outings."

"You let me know when and where and I'll avail myself to you, Mrs. Tate," Rachel finished. She had noticed that ever since she'd returned from Vegas, Dashawn's mom had changed a little. She'd always been nice to her, but now it seemed, as if she wanted to spend more time with her. *Wonder what's changing with Mrs. Tate, she seems motherly towards me suddenly. Hmm.* "So, what sounds good?" she inquired just as her phone rang with an unknown number that she let go to voicemail. But her phone rang right back with the same number forcing her to answer due to curiosity. "Hello. WHAT? OH GOD. I-I'M ON MY WAY!" she yelled as she got up quickly causing her chair to fall over.

"Oh my God, Rachel, what's the matter?" Mrs. Tate jumped up from the table to reach for her arm.

"I'm sorry Mrs. Tate. I gotta get to the hospital…" She started crying.

"Hospital? What's going on Sweetie?"

"My mom, my mom—oh God, my mom. She's gone, she's gone," she cried as she stumbled toward the exit of the restaurant.

"Oh no, I'm so sorry. Let me come with you and drive. First, let me pay for our drinks," she told Rachel's retreating back.

Rachel barely heard her as she kept replaying the hospital representative told her that her mother was dead. *What the hell happened?*

Dashawn rushed into the hospital in search of his mother and Rachel, worried out of his mind. Spotting his mother, he rushed over to her. "Where is she, Ma?"

"Honey, they had to give her something to calm her down. They also had to admit her because her blood pressure shot up so fast and so high, they were worried she might have a heart attack or stroke," his mother explained in a quiet voice. "She has to stay overnight for observation. I'm sorry after I called you, all of this happened, and I didn't want to worry you any more than I already had when you were trying to get home."

"Mother-fuck-me," he spat.

She made a face at his choice of words, but ignored them. "Now, you have got to calm down before you see her son, cause she's already holding on by a thin thread and if she sees you this upset, it will only do more harm," she finished while rubbing his back.

"Ok, ok. But I need to see her and hold her. She was just getting to the point that her decision to walk away from the toxic woman wasn't causing her tears. Now this shit. FUCK!" he yelled.

"I know son, but please pull yourself together. Come on, I'll take you to her room."

"Wait, did she see her mom? What happened, how did she even die?" he questioned.

"I'm sure she'll tell you more, but her mother had been released from the hospital and doing well, so she wasn't here all this time if that's what you're thinking. She came into the emergency room having been in an accident and they were unable to revive her. It seems as if she crossed two lanes of traffic and was hit by an eighteen-wheeler. She and the truck were the only ones on the freeway at the time. So thankfully, there weren't any other vehicles involved and the truck driver walked away without injury."

"Son of a bitch. What the fuck was she doing?" He shook his head distressed.

"I don't know and that's the part that I'm sure Rachel will share with you. Come on," she said walking toward the elevator.

Dashawn could hear Rachel sobbing from outside her door causing him to rush into the room and grab her while cautious of the IV in her arm. "I'm so sorry, Love." He kissed her softly.

"She's gone, she's gone. I didn't even get to say sorry or bye or—or, oh God — my mom is gone. I can't do this she's gone!" she cried hysterically.

"I know Rachel, I know," he said as he climbed in the bed and rocked her back and forth in his arms. "I'm sorry I wasn't here, but I'm here now."

"Ah, she's gone. I can't believe, my mommy is gone. I'm so sorry mommy!" she wailed.

The nurse came in and looked at Dashawn before she reviewed the monitor looking over Rachel's vitals. "Sir, can you see if you can calm her down? Her blood pressure is spiking, and we need to get it to come down. If it doesn't come down in the next ten minutes, we're gonna have to give her a Valium or something," she informed him.

"How about you give her something now because I doubt that she'll be able to calm down otherwise. She'll also need to sleep which probably won't happen without the aid of something!" he snapped at the nurse.

"Don't snap at this poor lady Dashawn, she's just doing her job," his mother entered the conversation.

"Please forgive me. I'm anxious and worried about Rachel which isn't your fault," he apologized to the nurse.

"No problem Sir. Let me go grab something for her after I check with the doctor since she was already given something when they admitted her. I'll be right back." The nurse left the room.

"She left me Dashawn, and do you know what they told me might have happened?" she asked him.

"What Love?" he asked looking down at her drenched tear-soaked face.

"T-They said that s-she was using her phone or about to use h-her phone. You know who she was calling? Me. My name was on her phone's display, she was about to call me and I'll never know what she was going to say. N-never…" she stuttered as she began crying harder.

"No, we won't Love, but you're gonna be okay," he tried saying before she yelled at him.

"NO, IT'S NOT. IT'S NEVER GONNA BE ALL RIGHT AGAIN!" she yelled and began punching his chest.

"Get it all out Rachel," he coaxed her as the nurse slipped in and inserted something into Rachel's IV, unbeknownst to her as she was distracted by her hysteria. "Alright, Love. I'm sorry," he said grabbing her hands and hugging her tighter. A few minutes later, he felt her settle down and get real still. As he looked down, he breathed a sigh of relief when he found her sleep.

"Watching you at this moment," his mother spoke quietly." I'm even surer that this woman was meant for you and you were meant for her. I'm so glad that you're here to get her through this hurdle, Son. I'm gonna head out while she's asleep unless you need me for any reason?"

"I completely forgot you were here and in the room Ma. I'm sorry. No, I think I have everything I need in my arms. I'm gonna stay right here to make sure she sleeps or at least stays calm. Thanks for everything Ma. I'll call you tomorrow." He leaned up slightly as his mother kissed his head.

"No thanks needed, I'm glad I was with her when she found out," she said as she leaned down to kiss a sleeping Rachel on her forehead. "Don't forget to call me, so I know how she's doing."

"Will do. Drive home safely. Love you."

"Love you more," she said blowing him another kiss as she left the room closing the door quietly.

CHAPTER SIXTEEN

Rachel woke up feeling as if her world had crumbled although she and her mother were recently estranged, she thought she'd have time. *I just needed more time she might have come around.* She felt warm and went to move but was restricted lifting her head she saw Dashawn's arms protectively wrapped around her. "Dashawn, honey, Dashawn?" she quietly got out her voice lower than she anticipated.

"Good morning Rachel. How are you feeling?" he hesitantly probed.

"Like my world has been paused. Where's my phone? I need to call my family, the girls, a funeral home, shit my mom's job," she choked out as tears began to fall.

"You need to breathe, calm down none of that has to be done this second. Breathe Love," he urged as her breathing increased causing the monitor to go haywire. "Calm down. Slow, deep breaths. That's it."

"But nobody knows that she died, and I'm her next of kin, so it's my job," she cried.

"Ok, I'll handle the calls. Just tell me who needs to be notified." He rubbed her back soothingly.

"But it should come from me. They'll expect it from me. Oh God, how am I going to get through this?" She dropped her head in his chest.

"You'll get through it because you're a strong woman and I'll be here every step of the way. I've got you Love." He hugged her to him hoping his strength would somehow seep into her.

As Rachel drifted back to sleep, Dashawn's emotions were going just as erratic as the monitors attached to her proclaimed hers emotions to be. His heart was crying with her, but he had to be the pillar of strength she needed. He wished he could remove the pain and even guilt she was feeling, but all he could do was comfort her through it. As he remained still to allow her to sleep, her phone began vibrating on the table. Carefully reaching for it, he noted that it was her cousin Charlene. "Morning Char," he greeted gruffly.

"Damn cousin, you sound like shit," she returned laughing.

"It's Dashawn, Char. Rachel is uh-indisposed at the moment. I was going to call you in a little bit.

"Dashawn what's going on? Where are you? Is my cousin all right? Is something wrong with Rachel?" she fired the questions in rapid succession.

"Shit, slow down the questions Charlene. Starting at the top, Rachel is in the hospital for observation purposes. I hate to tell you like this, but your Aunt Debra passed away last night. Rachel was with my mother and didn't handle the news well. They had to give her something. Can you call the rest of your family and the girls? Although, they might know since I was out of town with their husbands when my mom alerted me of the events," he finished taking a breath.

"Son of a fucking bitch. Motherfucking, cow dick sucking bitch!" she ranted.

"Are you okay? Take deep breaths, you good? Are you by yourself?" he quizzed as he heard her take gasping breaths.

"Oh my God, are you serious right now? I gotta call my Mom. How's Rachel? SHIT!"

"First off, Rachel is sleeping right now, and for the moment she's hanging in there. She's processed a ton of emotions since last night. I'm here, so don't worry about rushing to her. Just go to your mom to give her the news and ensure that she'll be all right. I'm going to push for them to release Rachel today with some anti-depressants or something that might help her sleep." Dashawn sighed as he looked at Rachel twitching in his arms.

"Fuck. Yes. I'll get back with you, and I'll make sure the girls know, she'll need them. But if I know those women, they're in transit which is probably why they didn't call me," Charlene finished sadly.

Before Dashawn could even respond, Rachel's door opened and in walked Kayla, Myles, Maisha, and Monica. "I think you're right about that, Kayla just walked in."

"Alright, take Rachel's phone, so she doesn't try to take on things today. You know her stubborn ass will attempt to start doing something."

"Yep, I'm on it. Let me chat with Kayla and them. Call me if you need me. Don't worry about your cousin, I got her," he informed her.

"Dashawn, how is she?" Kayla whispered looking at Rachel. "She seems to be sleeping fitfully right now. Did they give her something to help?"

"She's not resting. I'm sure she can hear everything going on and yes, they gave her something to help calm her down. It worked for a little bit last night, but she tossed, turned, and jumped all night."

"Thank you for being here for her," she expressed wiping tears from her face.

"Don't thank me. I love this woman. So I'll always be here for her in whatever capacity she needs. Let me see if I can get her to wake up," he said, lightly moving her to check her sleep versus awake state.

Rachel's response was to moan and squeeze him tighter.

"Don't bother her. I have nowhere to be so when she wakes, we'll be here. Can you tell me what happened?" Kayla asked repositioning Maisha on her lap, as she got comfortable on the couch.

"Sure thing, but there's one part of that causes the most pain for Rachel," he announced to the room, "and she'll have to inform you of that part." *Even in death, her mother is still fucking with my woman. I wish we knew what she was calling to say.*

A week later...

Rachel arrived at the funeral in a daze…. it didn't seem real. Her steps into the funeral home were slow and miscalculated as she almost tripped over the step into the building.

"Shit. Are you okay?" Dashawn asked as he quickly reached out to grab her and prevent her from falling.

Rachel couldn't respond, as her mind was a million miles away. She was suspended in the depths of grief and guilt. *If I had just been able to hold out longer, we would have never been separated. What could she have wanted to tell me so bad that she picked up her phone at that moment?*

"I'm not sure that she heard you or realized that she could have fallen Dashawn," her father Lee spoke growing concerned by the dazed look on his daughter's face.

"Honey, Ms. Spencer?"

Rachel looked around in confusion. "Huh?" she answered trying to fight past the thoughts swirling in her mind.

"We can take all the time you need before entering the room," the funeral director told her.

"I-uh, just need a-um-a minute. Where's your bathroom?" she asked the representative stepping away from whoever was standing close to her. She felt people around her, but she was too wrapped up in her head to notice.

"Down the hall to the left, Honey." Her Aunt Mae stepped in front of her to ask,

"Need me to go with you?"

"No ma'am. I'm-I'm fine..." Her voice cracked. She turned and made her way to the bathroom. Entering, she ran into the nearest stall locking the door. Leaning against it, she took a breath fighting the water from escaping her eyes. “Don’t you dare stand here and cry. Get it together,” she berated herself. The pain won as she thought about seeing her mother for the last time in a casket, no less. “Oh God, why did it end this way!” she yelled collapsing against the door sobbing loudly as the pain took over.

Dashawn was pacing back and forth in the lobby as he waited for Rachel to return from the bathroom. He couldn’t believe that she didn’t see the step going into the funeral home a few minutes ago. As she turned his way with the catch, he saw the haunted look on her face and knew that she was battling internal demons that prevented her from reality and they seemed to be winning.

His nerves, as well as his emotions, were spiraling haphazardly as he was defenseless against the grief and guilt she was feeling. Pacing continuously, he noticed it was taking a while for Rachel to come out and he turned toward the bathroom. Walking briskly in front of him was Reia with a determined yet stoic look on her face. “What’s going on?” he grumbled.

“I think you might need to follow me,” she responded, then turned and walked back toward where she’d come from.

When he entered the restroom a few minutes later, he heard the painful sobbing coming from a stall that her group of friends and cousin were standing guard in front of.

"I'm sorry, I'm sorry!" Rachel was saying over and over.

Jocelyn wiped tears from her own eyes to tell him, "We've been trying to get her to open the door, but I'm not sure if she hears us."

"Has she been like this all week Dashawn? Why didn't you call us to come in sooner?" Caressa cried.

"Kayla and I are here locally you didn't have to take this on by yourself," Charlene griped.

"Ladies, I know that you all wanted to be here, but SHE wouldn't let me call any of you. I only got access to her because I have a key to her house and she knows that I wouldn't be pushed away. You can all yell at me once we get her through this. Now, let me see if I can get her out of there." He sighed. As the women stepped away from the stall, he walked to it and gently spoke to Rachel, "Love, can you open the door please?"

Rachel continued crying and didn't react.

So, he decided to go into the empty stall next to hers. He stood on the toilet and climbed down into her booth, careful of the open toilet lid.

"Did his big ass really just climb into the stall with her?" Charlene asked in disbelief.

"He sure did, if this occasion were a different one, I would be giving him dap when he walks out. So, another time, another day," Caressa promised.

In the stall, Dashawn wrapped Rachel in his arms, kissed her hair and whispered, "I've got you, Rachel. You can do this. Your family and friends are here to support you through this. You've got to come out of here and I'll be right beside you every step of the way." He kissed her neck softly.

Rachel lifted her head slightly and gave him a subtle nod.

Grabbing some tissue, he dabbed at her face, careful not to rub her makeup off. Then he tore off more tissue and put it to her nose. "Blow for me Love." Once she was a little more presentable, he opened the door, following her to the sink. As he stood there washing his hands, he peeked at Rachel. He would have to keep watch over her today. When she was finished, he took her hand and walked with her out the door towards the parlor where her mother laid with her family following behind them.

Lord, give me the strength needed to be her strength.

Today has been an absolute nightmare, but I made it. Rachel rode home in the funeral home's family car, completely numb. Seeing her mom in that casket was gut-wrenching for her, but then all of this was painful. She wished she had an opportunity to reconcile with her mother or even find out what she might have been attempting to call and say. That was something that was causing her the most anxiety. Because of whatever prompted her to pick up her phone, she'd gotten herself killed, and she'd never know what was on her mind.

As she fidgeted in her seat, she felt Dashawn squeeze her hand a little tighter and she gave him a small twitch of her lips. She'd had a hard time smiling or feeling joy of any kind since the hospital called her a week ago. The funeral had been unbearable as her family members showed their asses as if they were so close to her mother. "Can you believe how my cousin Lana acted today?" she said before spacing back out into her head. "Oh, I have a poem I'd like to share when everyone gets to my house. I couldn't bring myself to do it at the service, but I will after a while," she again spoke to no one in particular.

"Ok, Love," Dashawn told her as he leaned over and kissed her lips lightly.

Arriving at her house, the funeral home attendant opened the door for her and waited for Dashawn to help her out of the car. Once she was in the house, she sat on the couch as she watched the man bring in vases and planters of flowers, before long her living room looked like a small flower shop. "Damn it all, these flowers can't stay here. Got me feeling like I need to take stock in Flowerama or some shit!" she spat angrily.

"You can send them with whoever you want. It's all right Love." Dashawn studied her pensively before speaking again, "Are you hungry, want anything to drink?"

"No, I'm ok…" She sighed.

"Okay, but in a little while, I want you to eat and drink something for me. I won't push right now, but I will later," he told her as he went to let in whoever was ringing the doorbell.

"Fine," she snapped.

A few seconds later, she was bombarded with company, her dad and all her friends were there with their husbands, her cousin Charlene came with her beau Mark, Charlene's mom, Aunt Mae, her assistant, Megan and a few people from work.

Rachel nodded at them all. "If you all don't mind, I want to read a poem I wrote. Although I'm not sure it's really a poem or just some words that I threw together. Anyway, I want to share it," she concluded. Before she could get up to grab the paper, she saw Dr. Hawkins walk into the room. "Oh, my goodness, Dr. Hawkins-Sharon, uh, I'm so sorry I forgot to call you. Who called you?" she sputtered.

"Aw, don't worry about it, Dashawn called me. Now it seems as if I'm right on time for this written piece you want to read. Grab it and we'll be ready whenever you are. Hello everyone," Dr. Hawkins stated and greeted the crowd with a wave of her hand.

Rachel walked back into the room, as everyone got quiet, she peered around making sure that everyone was there. "So, I don't want you to do anything but listen okay everyone? Um, I wrote this shortly after me and mom's separation so uh, it probably doesn't rhyme or isn't really a poem but um, it's what I was feeling at the time." She gripped the paper tightly as her eyes began to water.

"We're not going to judge your words Chelly, just go ahead and start whenever you're ready and we'll be completely quiet," her Dad said giving everyone in the room a nod before giving her a reassuring smile.

"Alright, here it goes," she said clearing her throat, and then began to read it aloud,

"*It's missing. My mother's love is missing.*

What do you do when the love you're supposed to feel from your mother is missing?

When life has delivered so many painful blows that breathing becomes difficult.

How do you process through a life that was given but never explained?

When you feel as if your very existence was her greatest mistake.

What do you do when the one thing you want, and need has never been given?

What do you do when the love of a mother was an image seemingly out of your reach?

When all you wanted is for her to love you, support you, hold you up, nurture you?

What do you do when accepting her mistreatment felt like receiving her love?

What do you do when you've grown comfortable with her rejection, hatred, and displeasure with your existence? What do you do when a mother's love is missing? You find your strength. You find your ability to overcome.

You find the you that you've always known was hidden behind the pain.

When a mother's love is missing... you search for God's perfect love for you.

Today, I will search for a love like I've never known before.

Today, I vow to find real love despite her love that is missing."

When Rachel finished reading, she took a deep breath and looked around the room. She noted that all her sister-friends, her cousin Charlene and her Aunt Mae were all crying. While the men had either drooped shoulders, wore slack expressions or they were rubbing their chests with an empty stare. The overwhelming sense of sadness was hugging her like a wet blanket, and she couldn't help but feel the loss of what would never be. "I uh—I, at the time I didn't expect for it ever to go anywhere but the paper that I'd written it on. But I think now is a fitting time for it. I'm sorry, I didn't mean to make anyone cry…" she stopped as she tried to wipe her face.

"It's ok Love. I'm glad that you were able to get it off your chest," Dashawn stated as he handed her some tissues while giving her a side hug.

"How about we talk about something else to lighten the energy in this room?" she tried to change the subject.

"You know it's okay to be in the moment, Chelly." Her father was hugging her as best he could with Dashawn only moving slightly out of the way. "Nobody will hold your emotions or feelings against you. You're entitled to every feeling that's coursing through you. Never apologize for how you feel." He leaned into her ear and whispered, "I'm so sorry Chelly, I wish I could make your pain disappear…" Then he kissed her cheek.

"Somebody please talk about something, anything else. All of this crying and high emotions are making me stay in the moment," she whined.

"How about we play charades?" Dr. Hawkins spoke up suggesting something that would allow everyone's focus to be diverted.

"That's a great idea, who wants to be on what teams?" Charlene asked. "I nominate Dashawn and Rachel have separate teams with each being a captain. Besides, if Dashawn gets any closer to her right now, nobody will get to touch her again." She busted out laughing helping to lighten the emotionally charged room.

Nearly an hour after reading her poem in front of the people gathered, Rachel sneaked out to her reading cove in the backyard and sat down in her chaise. She needed a minute to say a quick prayer and clear her head. Bowing slightly, she said a prayer that had been swimming in her mind since she wrote the poem.

God, those questions have plagued me for years. Those very questions I have asked after shedding many tears. I have to find strength and comfort in the one who sees the good in me. The one who reminds me that even in the midst of pain and sorrow life is worth it. The one who holds my hand, pierced my heart, and put a stamp of approval on my very existence. So today God, amid sadness, amid pain, I want to thank you for being my ONE. Thank you for being my comforter. Thank you for being my life preserver. Thank you for being the lifter of my head. Thank you for supplying my very needs. Thank you for sending so many people to remind me that I am loved, and I am worth it. Father, I just want to say, Thank You. I'm ready for real love now.

Once she said the last acknowledgment of thanks, she heard the lyrics of the gospel song *Free* echoing in her head. *My redeemer has saved me from sin... My soul is awakened, I live... Free from what held me... Free from what fought me.* The song had become an anthem of hers ever since she heard it which ironically happened to be the morning before the funeral. She smiled and leaned back in the chaise enjoying the quietness in her mind.

CHAPTER SEVENTEEN

What Rachel didn't know was that Dashawn had been standing watch over her the entire time.

He stood in the shadows, as he'd been worried about her throughout the day and even more so after she'd read her written piece in front of the crowded room. He knew that while she was pretending to have it together, she was only putting on a front for the sake of everyone. He'd seen the look in her eyes that caused his heart to weep and now, here she was trying to overcome everything.

After today, she'll never be this heartbroken again, if I have a say in the matter.

Trying not to get caught spying on her, he rushed back into the house. Not paying attention as he was looking behind him for Rachel, he bumped into a few bodies on his way in. "I guess I'm not the only one keeping close watch over her." He laughed as he noticed her dad, cousin, and friends gathered in the kitchen. "Quick, let's go into the living room. Act normal, otherwise she'll know something is up when she walks back in here," he stated as he led the group out of the kitchen.

"Who made this food, anything I need to watch out for?" Rachel yelled from the kitchen a few minutes later.

"Come sit down, Ms. Busy Body, one of us can get you something," Caressa yelled back.

“I can make myself a plate, besides I’m already in here. It doesn’t make sense to have someone else do it,” Rachel grumbled as she opened various lids.

“Now, you all have known her longer than I have, and I know better than that. That damn woman in there is stubborn as hell!” Dashawn laughed at the nods he got.

“I heard that Dashawn,” she spat as she slammed a lid.

“Wasn’t trying to hide it from you Love. Now come on and sit down. We can get you whatever you need.”

“Hmmph, what if what I need isn’t in this kitchen under these covered dishes…” She dropped her voice seductively.

“Hahaha, well then to that I say, what you need can be arranged. Matter of fact, how about I promise to take care of those needs privately when we’re alone?” he responded huskily.

“Mom, your niece done switched from grief-stricken to *NEED*Y in two point two seconds. She must have had quite the experience in that backyard.” Charlene snickered.

“Honey, I’m still trying to figure out if she and Dashawn forgot we were sitting in this damn room!” Reia giggled.

Dashawn was a lot of things, but embarrassed wasn’t one of them. It’d been a while since him and Rachel had been intimate. So if she was up for it, company be damned, he wasn’t about to walk away from an opportunity to promise her fulfillment.

Rachel didn't think people would ever go home. She even thought she'd have to kick them out of her house forcefully. She felt grateful for the love and support, but now she wanted to give some special attention to her man. He'd been her saving grace over the past week and she wanted to show him her gratitude in a way that they both could benefit from. "Thank you for everything that you did for me babe and before you say it… I know I don't have to thank you, but I am anyway. I want you to know that I don't take you for granted. Can you also thank your mother for me? I'm not sure I would have made it through that day if she hadn't been there. I love that you have her in your life, she's an amazing mother. She certainly raised a hell of a man. I love you with all my heart, Dashawn Sanders."

"Your support circle is bigger than you knew and I, for one, am grateful. I'll also tell my mother and I love you too, Rachel Spencer."

"I'm glad that we've gotten that out of the way, now I have another way that you can help me." She winked as she crawled in his lap.

"Oh, I like where this is going." He adjusted himself on the couch so she would be more comfortable.

"Why don't you take me to bed?" she purred then leaned in to kiss his neck.

"Yeah, I am feeling tired as well." He stood with her wrapped around his waist trudging toward her bedroom.

After laying Rachel on the bed, Dashawn stroked her cheekbone and lips lightly. He took his thumb and rubbed it over the bridge of her nose-tweaking it before he leaned down and sucked Rachel's lips into his mouth. The action caused her to moan. Gazing into her eyes, he undressed her slipping the dress over her head. Her nipples hardened into pebbles once he unclipped the purple bra she was wearing. Taking one of her breasts into his hand, he pulled it to meet his mouth and sucked so hard she was sure he thought it contained his next meal.

Pushing him backward not wanting to prolong this long overdue coupling, she started to remove his clothing. She pulled his underwear off with her teeth and took his dick into her mouth as she savored the tangy sweetness. Licking all around the shaft of his cock with her tongue, she took his balls in her mouth and sucked gently.

This action caused him to shudder. "Fuck, ooh Love, we got all night. Come here and sit on my face," he moaned out.

Straddling his face, Rachel held onto the headboard as he licked her front to back sucking her clit into his mouth. "Oooh, baby just like that" she purred. *There is nothing more beautiful than your man sucking your clit with excitement and appreciation for the act.*

Dashawn feasted on Rachel's clit as he enjoyed the juices oozing out of her. "Damn, you taste good."

"I need you inside of me," she panted trying to hold off her orgasm. Rachel tried moving off his face, but

Dashawn sucked her in his mouth harder causing her to explode. “Shiiitttt!” she screamed out.

“Mmm,” he said licking his lips, lifting her up and placing her on his dick.

Rachel grimaced as she adjusted to the feeling of Dashawn slowly moving inside of her. It had been a while since they had sex with everything going on but since his tongue was inside of her minutes before, she was slick. A few minutes into his stroking, Dashawn began to pick up his pace, and she met him stroke for stroke. As he stroked up, she thrust down creating a synced rhythm. Taking hold of his hands, she clasped them together and rode him harder.

“I missed that part of our relationship, but I wasn’t going to bother you until you were ready. I’m happy that you made your request known,” he breathed out ruggedly a few minutes after their joint climax. “How about we take a bath? It’ll further relax you.” He shifted lightly laying her on the bed to go fill the tub.

A few minutes later, Rachel drowsily opened her eyes as Dashawn lifted her carrying her into the bathroom. He climbed in with her sinking down into the water as she leaned back on his chest exhaling from the comfort of the water’s heat. *I could spend my life, right here at this moment, doing this very thing with this very man.*

As the sunlight hit his face, Dashawn opened his eyes and looked at the woman lying beside him. He loved everything about her, her quirks, her stubborn streak, her attitude— he loved everything. He felt as if today was the day to seal the deal and secure his future. Gingerly, Dashawn exited the bed, he was gonna make her breakfast, but first duty called. After taking care of his business, he checked to see that Rachel was still sleeping, so he tiptoed out of the room and to the kitchen.

Damn, I should have gone to the store while everyone was here. Oh well, guess its omelets and toast.

Fifteen minutes later, Dashawn carried a tray back to the room. He'd made Rachel an omelet with spinach, tomatoes, mushrooms, and cheese, sliced bananas, strawberries, toast and fresh squeezed orange juice. "Rise and shine, my sleeping beauty." He leaned down to kiss her lips after he placed the tray at the end of the bed.

"Isn't this a surprise, thank you Dashawn! Good morning to you too. You didn't have to do this," Rachel said as she returned his kiss noting the tray of food.

"Uh, we've had this discussion before Love, I know I didn't, but I wanted to. You deserve to wake up like this every morning. Now come on, sit up so you can eat before your food gets cold. I also would like to monopolize your day, but I understand that you need to spend time with the girls before they leave. However, dinner will be spent with me and me alone, so lock me in now," he told her as he positioned the tray in front of her.

"So, how are you handling everything? Are you doing ok?" Reia asked sipping her cocktail.

Rachel nodded. "I'm uh, taking it slow for now, part of me is harboring some guilt, and the other part wishes I knew what she would have said."

Charlene shook her head. "Well, you need to concern yourself with things that you can control only and since none of us knows what Aunt D would have said you can't spend time worrying about it. Shit, for all we know, she was going to project more foul shit onto you."

Jocelyn nodded. "That's true. You shouldn't spend time beating yourself up about that mystery. It will cause you to go crazy if you continue on this path."

"Have you talked to Dr. Hawkins about these feelings you're having?" Caressa asked.

Rachel let out a sigh. "I know that I shouldn't spend time on it and I know that it's beyond my control, but I can't help how I feel. I also hate that we fell out and something happened so soon after it makes me feel like a horrible daughter. To answer your question, I haven't seen Dr. Hawkins since she was here after the funeral. I didn't keep my appointment after my mom passed and it didn't seem appropriate to pull her to the side for a house call," she finished.

"Girl, please," Reia retorted. "I'm pretty sure she's had worse situations and didn't she already make a house call for you before? She probably expected you to have her ducked off in a corner somewhere."

"Anyway, let's change the subject, cause I only have limited time with you all. Dashawn insists that I have dinner with him. So, let's figure out how to make this time count shall we?" She smirked.

"Hmmph, the old ball and chain speaks, and suddenly you turn into Mary-fucking-Poppins? I see how you are, dissing your girls for some dick," Charlene whisper yelled.

They all laughed.

After dinner, Dashawn turned on iHeart radio choosing a station that would play music that was light and romantic. He had candles lit all around the house, but he decided for them to relax on the couch in the living room. It had been a rough couple of days and relaxation was something that he knew Rachel needed. He also wanted to just enjoy a quiet evening with the woman who held his heart. As Rachel leaned on his chest holding his hands, Promise to Love began playing. "May I have this dance Love?" he softly asked as he stood up taking her with him.

Blushing she nodded as she walked into his arms.

Wrapping her in his arms, pulling her close he began swaying.

Dashawn crooned the words in her ear as he held her tight, loving how she fit in his arms and his embrace. The ring he'd picked out with his mother's help sat snuggly in his pocket. He just needed the right opportunity to ask her. This song and this moment was a perfect set up. Spinning her around, he subtly dropped to one knee as he eased the ring out of his pocket.

Rachel gasped when she realized that Dashawn was on bended knee holding a ring. “Uh— Dashawn?”

“This poetic genius had no idea that when he wrote this song, it would be the inspiration for this moment in OUR lives, but as I genuinely listened to and digested the words, I knew that he and I had something in common. You see, I promise to love you. You are what I needed to compliment my life. You are the front to my back. You are my assurance that there is something in this world worth living for. So today, I promise to love you for the rest of our lives. Rachel Spencer, will you do me the honor of becoming my wife?”

Rachel just stood there as her eyes dripped with tears. “Oh, my God! Dashawn you want to marry me?” she asked seemingly surprised.

“Love…marrying you is what I was created for. Now, before my knees fall asleep will you answer me?” he smirked.

“Oh baby, I’m sorry. Hell yeah, I’ll marry you!” she replied as she fell into him causing them to land on the floor.

Dashawn kissed her while feeling elated that she agreed to be his wife and spend the rest of her life with him. “Thank you, Rachel,” he told her slipping the ring that she hadn’t paid much attention to onto her finger.

CHAPTER EIGHTEEN

Rachel was finally getting back to somewhat normal then the call she'd received from the attorney who had her will a few weeks after the funeral almost tilted her balance of sanity again.

"Hi, I'm looking for Rachel Spencer," a raspy male voice probed.

"Uh, this is she. May I ask who this is?"

"My name is Frank Johns, and I'm the attorney for Debra Carpenter. It's my understanding that Ms. Carpenter has passed away?" the man asked.

"Yes, she has so why are you calling me now, I've already done the funeral," Rachel stated growing frustrated by the call.

"Ma'am, I don't mean to upset you, I'm in possession of your mother's will, and I'd like for you to come by my office to go over it," he posed.

"Now, is not a good time for me, can we go over it right now this way?" she asked.

"I suppose that's alright, uh as your mother's immediate next of kin I wanted to let you know that everything that she owns is yours except her residence. With that being the case, I need for you to go clean out her house so that we can turn it over to the person whom she left it to," he said slowly.

"What do you mean, the person she left it to? Isn't that person me? I don't understand," she inquired.

"I'm sorry I can't relay that information to you, all I can say is that I need you to go over to the house by seven o'clock tonight. If you're unable to do so, I can check with the new homeowner to see if they'll hold off on taking possession of the residence," he finished.

"Man, you sure don't waste any time, let me just rearrange my life to accommodate your inconvenience. I'll go over today," she grumbled hanging up the phone.

Arriving at the house nearly two hours later, she entered but paused quickly as her mother's fragrance surrounded the dwelling and almost caused her to break down from memory. Holding onto the wall she said, "Mom. It's so weird to be here, and you're not." Proceeding on through the house, she looked around trying to decipher if there was anything that she wanted to take or keep as a souvenir, but her emotions began to overtake her, she was struggling to catch her breath as tears streamed down her face. "Damn, all I can see is bad memories and heartache in this house. Jesus, give me strength." Ten minutes later, she stood inside her mother's bedroom, where she saw a pill bottle of Lithium "Hmmph, why on earth does my mother have a prescription for Lithium?" And a note on her nightstand. Approaching it, she noted that the letter appeared to be a diary entry type thing from the day she died, picking it up she began to read her mother's words.

I'm laying here wondering where I went wrong in this life, everything has gone to shit, and I've only tried to be a good person. Hell, it's not my fault that my damn daughter can't do anything right. Every time I look at her, I see what a disappointment my life became. Looking at her causes me so much damn pain. I really wish she would've died along with the other bastard that was overtaking my fucking body. I know I shouldn't feel that way about my own child, but I lost everything because of her birth. Thank heavens, I only had her little ass, so my life can continue knowing that I've finally succeeded in driving a permanent wedge between us. She's much better off without me that's for sure. I can't believe Dr. Derick says that I'm bipolar, of all fucking things. I'm not crazy, and I won't apologize for my feelings. I'm not about to take these stupid ass pills. He can kiss my ass wanting to have a joint session with my daughter. How dare he? She doesn't need to know a damn thing and certainly not his dumb ass diagnosis. Like him, she can kiss my ass since she's so fucking done with me. Fuck her. Yes, one day, she'll regret the decision and I'll have the last laugh.

Unable to read any more, she dropped the note and numbly left the room. She could have fucking told her mother that she was bipolar herself. Nobody has those types of moods and irrational behavior traits while being normal. "I've got to get out of here. None of this shit is worth taking. Why am I even here? Let the new owner clean this shit out." Walking off the front door, she stumbled to see HIM standing in the driveway leaning against a late model Chevy Impala.

Here was the man that caused her life to spiral out of control at nine years old. How could her mother still be messing around with him after all these years? Patrick

Walker was the man her mother had been sleeping with the night her father caught her cheating. *Oh God, please tell me that my eyes are playing tricks on me.* But his words confirmed that she saw clearly.

"Hey Lil bit, although seems like I should be calling you big thickness now," he mocked.

"How about I call you 'dead to me' motherfucker? What the fuck are you doing in my mother's driveway with your bitch ass?" she growled.

"You mean, my driveway. This is my house now. I was still blowing Debra's back out behind late-night doors. Guess she finally decided to reward me for my efforts," he bragged popping his t-shirt.

"Sonofabitch!" Rachel yelled as she stormed past him to her car.

She vowed to forget about it, as the house was nothing but walls full of bad memories. He could have it.

Five weeks later…

Rachel was listening to iHeart radio two months after her mother died and the gospel song *Free* came on. She hadn't brought herself to listen to it since before the funeral, but the lyrics had tears raining down her face. The song spoke to her on multiple levels, and she couldn't help but respond every single time. *I'm at work and shouldn't be sitting here crying.* As she repeated the song as soon as it ended she made herself a reminder on her phone to go to iTunes when she got home to purchase it. She hadn't been affected by a song in a long time, but these lyrics struck her profoundly causing her to pause for a few minutes while she processed her emotions.

The song reminded her even though she had periods where her grief was consuming that freedom was hers. Looking at her hand, she still smiled at the beautiful engagement ring she'd received from Dashawn. The ring was a 3-carat princess-cut diamond frame vintage-style twist. It was stunning and made her snicker every time her eyes glanced at all the sparkle. Even though her mood was momentarily dampened by the memory of her mother, remembering the night Dashawn proposed always changed her attitude. Laughing, she remembered calling her girls over to her house the next day to let them into her blissful moment…

…"Hey ladies, come on in. Rachel will be out in a few," she heard Dashawn say.

"Girl, bring your ass, how you got us over here and not be ready?" Charlene was complaining.

"Uh Rachel, our flights are a few hours away, come on!" Reia yelled.

Rachel was trying to find something to distract her ring, but she decided to just go with it. Walking quickly into the dining room where she was serving brunch she joyfully stated, "I'm getting married, who's hungry?"

Collective gasps were heard around the room followed by several—"What? Come again?"—responses.

"Now, come on Love you can't just leave them hanging like that. Got me feeling like yesterday's leftovers and like you're ashamed of me," Dashawn spoke up smiling.

"I want to know the playback!" Charlene asked a little stunned. "Did you just announce that you're getting married?"

"Only in true Rachel fashion, do you inform your closest friends of such exciting news. Spill the Spencer tea!" Jocelyn deadpanned.

"Right, I need information because we were all just together yesterday afternoon..." Caressa stopped looking at Rachel with raised eyes.

"Alright, alright, calm down. After dinner last night, Dashawn proposed presenting me with this stunner!" Rachel boasted showing her left hand containing her ring.

Monica slapped the table to say, "Well damn, I've said it once, and it deserves an encore, that cruise vacation was one for the record books. Two of you went single but came home with love and husbands. I think we should take another cruise!"

"Girl, why are you slapping that table like it owes you money? Kayla, get your sister in law!" Caressa laughed.

Rachel smirked as she looked at the crazy facial expression Monica was wearing. "I'm not sure about Kayla, but I didn't set out to obtain love on that vacation. I wanted a booty call," she said moving away from Dashawn in case he was offended by her response.

"Shit, me too it just became so much more than that," he declared as his face lit up with happiness and love in his eyes.

"Aww, he's *so* sprung," Charlene singsonged teasing Dashawn.

"Hmmph, hard to be sprung when you've—never mind," he said realizing that he wasn't talking in his head.

"Poor baby, all backed up. I thought I took care of you. We can ask them to leave and I can handle business," Rachel promised.

"Really? Dick that good you willing to diss us?" Charlene continued.

At that, everyone began hooting as they shook their heads at Charlene's banter.

"Not dissing you but if my man needs some TLC, then…" Rachel shrugged.

"Nah, I'm good Love for a half hour maybe. Come on fellas, let's head out back and leave these women to their antics," Dashawn said to the seemingly mute men in the room.

Rachel enjoyed spending time with her friends before everyone had to go back home. She knew that they'd see each other again soon, but in times like these, she wished they lived closer. Even though she and Kayla worked together and lived not far from each other, their relationship changed once she got married and now that she was a mother. She didn't realize how much things would change until now. The realization occasionally made her sad, but she dispelled those feelings and got up to do something productive. *Might as well start plotting out my wedding.*

Dashawn sat at work trying to be productive since he'd taken off with Rachel, his work had piled up a little, and it had taken him these last two months to dig out. *Man, get your head in the game.*

"Hey Sanders, how are things?" his boss inquired from his doorway.

"Going smooth Mr. Keener. Anything in particular you need?"

"Straight to the point I see. I'm here to tell you that I need you to go to a conference in Denver. You'll need to be gone for three weeks. The conference is a week and then I need you to check on things at our office out there. I've been hearing some things that have caused me to be a little antsy. For now, I won't disclose the information, but I need your eyes and ears open," his boss finished.

"Uh, sure thing. When do I need to leave?" Dashawn asked hoping he had time to spend with Rachel before he'd be gone.

"Well, that's the unfortunate part, I need you there tomorrow. Joan has already booked your flight and made hotel arrangements for you. Sorry, for the late notice man, but it couldn't be helped. I have to run to a meeting, so call me once you get to Denver tomorrow and I'll give you an update on the situation."

"Alright, if you don't mind I'm going to get out of here, so I can get prepared," Dashawn stated trying not to show his aggravation.

"No problem, chat soon." Then his boss left.

"How in the hell did I get blindsided with this bullshit?" he griped as he shut down his computer and prepared to leave his office. *How am I going to tell Rachel I'm leaving?* Hearing his phone ringing from his pocket, Dashawn answered before his voice mail picked up. "Just the beautiful woman I was thinking about. How's your day going?"

"You're sweet, it's going, but I'm going to back work tomorrow. I'm done sulking and am ready to start living again," Rachel optimistically replied.

"You sure? What's Dr. Hawkins and Kayla saying?"

"I don't need permission to return to work from anybody but myself. I'm fine, okay," she replied.

Dashawn hesitated for a few minutes, Rachel had been on family leave since her mother passed away and he wasn't sure if she was ready, but he wasn't about to say that. Instead, he said, "Alright Love, as long as you're sure, I support your decision. I was um, about to call you though. I uh, gotta go out of town. Um, this time for three weeks. I'm heading home to pack now as I leave early tomorrow morning," he rushed out.

"Okay," came her quick response.

"I know I'm—ok? Is that all you're going to say?" he asked surprised.

"Yeah, your job requires you to travel sometimes. My job is to be understanding," she nonchalantly stated.

"Hmm. Ok, I'll call you when I get things together. Can you come over? I need to see you before I leave."

"I bet I know which part of you wants to see me more. But yeah, call me and I'll come over. I'll bring dinner *and* dessert." She laughed wickedly.

He grinned at this. “Deal. See you soon, Love.”

Rachel was a little annoyed with Dashawn by the time she showed up at his house and her annoyance clouded her judgment to the point that she almost forgot he was leaving in the morning. “Hey,” she grumpily greeted him as he opened the door for her.

“So, I take it that you’re not happy with me right now?” He took in her downturned face and stiff shoulders.

“What gave you that impression?” she fired back.

“That right there gave me the impression, but I’m not sure I know what I did wrong. You want to enlighten me or are you gonna continue shooting daggers at me?” he asked as she stomped into the house.

“What gives you the right to question me or act as if I’m some fragile person who can’t handle her own affairs? I’m capable of making decisions for myself without needing someone else to respond for me,” she ranted swinging her arms in her frustration. She was so mad that she hadn’t acknowledged the look on Dashawn’s face.

“Okay, I’m not about to do this shit. It’s not how I want to leave you either, so can you put this unnecessary ass argument aside long enough for us to enjoy each other’s company before I’m gone? Did you hear me tell you earlier that I’ll be gone for three weeks? I don’t have time to argue nor do I want to argue with you. Come on Love, this isn’t what we do…” He sighed.

She hung her head she didn't want to argue with him either, but she also wasn't happy about his questions earlier. But she had to stop pouting and acting immature, he was about to leave town and she certainly didn't want to leave things in disarray beforehand. "I'm sorry Dashawn," she apologized walking over to stand in front of him.

"Let me clear something up. I know you're capable of deciding what's best for you but sometimes, you put others before yourself and I want to make sure that you're ready to return. Kayla is your boss, so I was asking from that perspective, and Dr. Hawkins is who's guiding you through this transition. I meant nothing by my inquiry and I'm not about to do this with you. Don't make waves that aren't rocking, alright?" He now sounded aggravated.

"Fine, can we change the subject?"

"Well, now that you're all pissy and in your feelings, I think you need to be in yoni-out." He smirked wrapping his arms around her.

"Yoni-out? What are you talking about?" she questioned.

"It's time out for down there." He gestured to between her thighs.

"Fuck that shit! You're about to be gone for weeks and you want to put her in time out? You done lost your ever-loving mind, bring your ass we've got to get stored up for this separation," she told him dragging him toward his bedroom by his belt loops as he boisterously laughed the whole way.

CHAPTER NINETEEN

Dashawn sat in his hotel room three weeks later having just hung up the phone with his boss. His time in Denver was being extended for another three weeks, and he was pissed but unable to do anything about it. Gotta call the firecracker with this shit, not gonna win me any more points. "Hey Love, how are you?" he said when Rachel picked up her phone.

"Not too good, but I'm sure it's nothing. How are you, where are you, you heading to the airport?" she rapidly inquired.

He hesitated before answering, "I'm sorry, but I'm still in Denver, turns out my boss needs me to stay out here another three weeks."

"What? Why? You've already been there three weeks, shit!" she stopped on a deep exhale.

"I know but there's an issue with our office out here, there may be some illegal activity going on is all I can share. So since I'm in a management position, I need to do some investigating and talking with employees. It's not the best situation, but I'll be home as soon as I possibly can. Now what's wrong with you?"

"I'm fine really, just a little bug. I miss you though," she groaned into the receiver.

"I miss you too. A bug? How long have you been feeling this way?"

"I don't know I haven't been paying much attention and I'm sure it'll pass. Unfortunately, I need to get back to work so how about I call you later on, once I get settled for the night. I think Charlene and I are going out tonight for happy hour," she rushed on.

"Why is it that you and your cousin seem to go out when I'm out of town or something? You better be rocking that bling you got a few weeks ago. Don't make me have to send out spies to whoop ass while I'm gone."

"Oh stop. I'm wearing my ring and I'm an engaged woman, spoken for and all that jazz," she teased.

"So that you know," he replied.

"No worries babe. Your position is fully secured," she stated in a deadpan voice.

"Now that we have that resolved, where are you two going? Mark hasn't vetoed Charlene's outing." He quickly laughed at the thought.

"Yeah, tasted like vinegar coming out, didn't it? We both know nobody tells or makes my cousin do ANYTHING unless they want that swift left...." she finished snickering.

"Yeah, Mark definitely has his work cut out for him."

"Right and he's crazy about her which makes me question *his* mental status."

"Damn, I miss you, Love. I'm sorry about this, we should start planning the wedding, but we haven't discussed a date yet. When would you like to lock me down?" he taunted.

"Uh, let me get back to you on that. So, how's your mom?" she asked in an attempt to change the subject.

"Waiting for us to communicate our wedding date. And don't think that I didn't notice you trying to change the subject. How about I have her call you and you two can do lunch or dinner?"

"That sounds like a great idea. Call her and have her give me a call when she's free."

Rachel gradually and cautiously took bites of her homemade Panini in hopes of not regurgitating it. Over the past two weeks, she'd been nauseous by everything, just this morning she swallowed her spit, and it caused her to fly to the toilet. She needed to be careful since she was at Dashawn's mom's house. After talking to him, his mom called and set up this lunch date but opted to host her in her home, instead of them going out. With each passing minute, her stomach grew queasier while knowing she wasn't going to make it much longer. "Uh, excuse me, Mrs. Tate, I need to use your bathroom." She quickly got out and hurried to the downstairs bathroom where she lost her breakfast and lunch. Coming back into the dining room a few minutes later, Dashawn's mom had a concerned look on her face.

"Are you all right Sweetie? Dashawn told me that you had a bug, but that was two weeks ago. Have you been to a doctor?" she quizzically asked.

"I'm fine and I haven't been to see my doctor yet. I'm sure it'll pass," she stated without meeting her eyes.

"I'm sure Dashawn and I will feel better if we knew with certainty that you were all right," Mrs. Tate said.

“There’s nothing for either of you to worry about. I’ll be okay,” Rachel reiterated.

“Why don’t you call your doctor now and make an appointment? I’d feel much better,” she pushed.

“Ok, ok.” Rachel snatched her phone out of her purse dialing her doctor’s office. “Afternoon, this is Rachel Spencer I need an appointment with Dr. Mars, please. Uh, I’ve been fighting some type of bug for a couple of weeks. I suppose I can, alright see you in a little while.”

“What’s going on?” Mrs. Tate inquired.

“I have to be in the office in the next hour, so can we reschedule?” Rachel requested.

“If you don’t mind I’d like to come with you, that way I can assure Dashawn if he calls,” Mrs. Tate said unmoving.

“I really don’t think you need to accompany me to my doctor’s office. I’ll let your son know what the doctor says if there’s a cause for alarm. Don’t worry I’m sure it’s nothing,” Rachel affirmed.

“Fine, but can you call me so that I know you’re as fine as you keep telling me you are?” Mrs. Tate persisted.

In a conference room in Denver, Dashawn listened to one of the firm’s managers outline some issues that had come up. He had been here for five weeks and was set to be here another week. He was tired of hearing these same complaints. His boss charged him with this investigation, but he wanted to go home. There were moments that caused him to hate his position in the company.

"On the night in question, what happened Cliff?" he asked. "You've been telling me everything but what I need to know. Are you conspiring against this company? If so, I will have your ass bounced out of this room before you can form your next lie. Now cut the bullshit!" Dashawn angrily spat. Then his phone began buzzing and with a quick glance, it showed his mother's number. Excusing himself, he answered, "Hey Ma, I'm kind of in the middle of something. Can I call you back?" he whispered.

"As soon as humanly possible, it's important," his mother declared.

"The last time you said that I had to hop on a flight, so another life, and death situation? Is Rachel good? I haven't heard from her in a week and was gonna call her this evening," he worried.

"Uh, it's a matter of life but not death this time. Just call me when you get time, it'll wait until then," she uttered and then disconnected.

Turning to face the man still sitting at the table looking sheepish, he stated, "Cliff, I don't have time to play these games with you. SO you have exactly ten minutes to tell me what I need to know or I'm firing your ass and having your shit cleaned out of here!" Dashawn growled.

Not long after this, Dashawn was calling his boss, "Mr. Keener, I just concluded my conference with Cliff and his story corroborates the one that everyone else had. How should we proceed?"

"Sanders, it's time to clean house, and I need you there to do it. You can come home next week I need you to finish this thing. I'll email over to you a list of people for you to sack," his boss rumbled.

"Alright," Dashawn barked. He was agitated even more now because he was told he had to stay through next week. With a deep breath, he returned his mother's call, "Ma, what's going on?"

"Son, I know you're busy, so I wasn't expecting you to call me back so fast…" His mother heaved a sigh.

"Ma, I'm under a lot right now, and I'm not in the mood to do this with you. What's going on?" he snarled.

"Let me tell you something Dashawn Sanders, I don't give a damn what you're under, don't be snarling and snapping at me!" she shouted.

"I'm sorry, but what is it?" he requested.

"When are you coming home? Maybe it can wait till then."

"Mr. Keener won't let me come home until I resolve this problem we have, so I'll be back next week probably towards the weekend. Now, what's going on? You're making me nervous."

"Have you talked to your fiancé?"

"I told you earlier, it's been a week, why?" he questioned.

"Call her!" she exclaimed then disconnected the call.

Damn that woman. She always did this to him!

Rachel hugged the toilet for the umpteenth time since coming home from the doctor. *It's like ever since the news was made known, you've been making your presence known baby. I hope this isn't going to be how your treat me when you're born.* Her phone sounded as soon as she rinsed her mouth. She then answered, "Char, now is not a good time."

"What the hell is going on that it's not a good time?" her cousin fussed.

"Char, as much as I love you… right now is NOT a good time!" she yelled ending the call as she ran back into the bathroom emptying her stomach again. The ringing of her phone caused her to grow very aggravated. "What the fuck Char?" she roared into the phone.

"I'm not Char, Love. What's got you so upset?" Dashawn stated.

"Dashawn?" Rachel was surprised to hear his voice.

"Besides, Charlene, who else are you expecting? What's going on, Rachel? Talk to me," he affirmed. "We haven't talked in a week and I was coming for you today anyway, but I'm sensing there's some shit going on there. Now you can either tell me, or I'll sacrifice losing my currently frustrating ass job and fly home," he promised angrily.

"Don't. Hold on." She dropped the phone and dry heaved into the toilet. Picking the phone up again, she spoke, "I'm sick at the moment, so how can I say this?"

"From the sounds of your dry heaving, either you're extremely sick, dying or you're pregnant, which is it?" he probed.

Rachel started crying unable to answer the question as she sat there immobilized with fear of his response. They hadn't planned on getting pregnant, they hadn't talked about it and while they hadn't prevented it from happening, she still wasn't sure of his response. So, she sat there crying softly until she heard him calling her name.

"Which is it, Love?" he pleaded.

"I-I-I'm sorry Dashawn," she cried.

"Sorry for what? What are you apologizing and crying for Rachel? Can you answer my question, please?"

"I'm pregnant Dashawn. I'm crying and apologizing because you didn't ask for this!" she whimpered.

"No, *we* didn't, but I'm not mad about it happening. We never talked about it, but we also haven't prevented it either. We're in this together and have you forgotten that you're no longer my girlfriend but my fiancé? We're getting married, Love and this pregnancy isn't going to change that. Now, how far along are you? I hate that I'm not there to wrap you in my arms right now."

"Thank you, Dashawn, I needed that reassurance. I'm not sure how far along I am. I was going to wait until you returned to see my OB. When will you be home babe?" she whined.

"Nah, don't wait, go ahead, call your doctor tomorrow, and get an appointment. I want them to make sure everything is okay with you and the baby. I'll do my best not to miss anything else if it's before I return. I have to stay until next week. So most likely, I won't be home until Friday night or Saturday morning."

"Ok, I do need to go see the doctor because this damn nausea is wearing me out. I haven't been able to keep much down," she informed him.

"I'm sorry I can't be there to make it better for you or do something for you," he said.

"You're doing something is what got me into this predicament in the first place, so I think you've done enough at the moment," she teased.

"We'll see about that when I get home. Now, why don't you go rest and call me tomorrow? I've got to head out of here and back to my hotel. If you get up later, then call me tonight. I love you Rachel Spencer, soon to be Sanders…" He kissed into the phone.

"I love you too Dashawn Sanders soon to be husband…" She returned kissing into the phone gingerly scared to cause any waves with the little person already demanding her body.

Dashawn was happy and smiling from ear to ear. Damn, he was gonna be a father. *She's having my baby.* Needing to clear the air, he dialed his mother. "I talked to Rachel, Ma," he declared when she answered after a couple of rings.

"And?" his mom asked.

"I think you know, so how about you tell me?" Dashawn quizzed.

"I'm going to be a grandma, although we need to find another name," she replied.

"How do you keep knowing the important events in my lady's life before I do, Ma? And it's always when I'm out of town and unlike last time, I can't rush back… without consequences, that is."

"Sometimes, God knows you need a representative, so he sends me in your place knowing that I will look after your treasured one as much as you would if you were here. So, how do you feel about the news?"

"I'm grateful for you Ma and I'm elated, but I wish I were there. She seems to be really sick. She had to keep putting the phone down and after a while, she was just dry heaving."

"The suffering of morning sickness, you'll have to just keep an eye on her to ensure that she doesn't need a closer monitoring by the doctor. Gotta run son, love you, and I can't wait for this next journey!"

"Alright, love you too Ma and neither can I." He smiled as his mother hung up. Dashawn stared blankly for a minute thinking how much his life was about to change. Wonder if she'd want to get married before the baby arrives?

Sitting in the exam room waiting for her doctor two days later, Rachel fought her stomach and sickness. *Damn, come on I've already thrown up multiple times this morning. This can't be how this whole fucking pregnancy is going to go. Ugh.* Dr. Montgomery walked into the room just as she felt another wave hit her "Oh, shit!" She jumped down from the table and ran to the nearest trash can holding her mouth.

"Oh, well I guess I don't need to ask why you're here. Good morning Rachel." Dr. Montgomery smiled.

"It hasn't been so good for me yet, but uh hey Dr. Montgomery, how's life treating you? I feel like I need to post up in an on-call room or something," she jested feeling a little weak.

"I take it you're pregnant, when did you find out?"

"Two days ago. I'd been feeling sick and fatigued for a few weeks now. At the insistence of my soon to be mother in law, I went to see my family doctor who shocked the shit out of me with the news."

"So, was this not a planned pregnancy? I know you haven't been taking any form of birth control," Dr. Montgomery stated washing her hands.

"Doc, my life has been so damn chaotic lately that my boyfriend turned fiancé and I just had sex for the first time three months ago after I can't even tell you how long. Were my damn eggs just sitting there flagging his sperm down or something? Shit." She sighed.

Laughing, Dr. Montgomery shook her head. "Well, I don't know about all that, but why don't we check and see how far along you are and just make sure everything is going okay. Hop back up on the table for me."

"Fine, but you might want to give me a bag or basin or something because it seems like every five minutes, I'm spewing," Rachel ranted as she climbed back onto the table.

Dashawn was on his way out of his hotel heading to the office when his phone rang, pausing for a minute, he saw Rachel's face. "Good morning Love," he greeted happily.

"Oh, it's NOT a good morning for me. I'm just leaving the doctor and I've thrown up more times than I can count. On top of that, I'm three months pregnant with fucking twins. When you do something Mr. Sanders, you do it! Making sure you make a damn statement in the process. What the fuck am I going to do with two babies at one damn time?" she spat.

"Twins? Did you say you're pregnant with t-twins?" Dashawn stuttered into the phone shocked by the news.

"Hell yeah, and I'm freaking out, so it's not time for you to boast or brag Mister!" she continued.

"Ok, ok, calm down this can't be good for my babies." He smirked and popped his suit collar even though she couldn't see him.

"Calm down? You want me to calm down AFTER I find out that I'm being invaded by body snatchers who will take my thick and make it thicker? This is some straight bullshit, ut-w-wait…" she stopped, and he could hear her getting sick in the background.

Damn. "You all right, Love?" he hesitantly asked.

"No, my body is not my own!" Rachel began crying as her emotions spiraled.

"Why are you crying?"

"Fuck, if I know. You might be ready to kill me six months from now at this rate. Then, you'll have two babies instead of one. What about getting married? You won't marry me now that you got two kids with one shot. Damn, we hadn't been intimate in forever and our return to the sack resulted in my upchucking repeatedly…." she sobbed helplessly as her emotions completely took over.

Dashawn held the phone wondering what happened to his feisty spitfire as this crying babbling woman wasn't her. "Um, I'm sorry Love. I'll be home next week."

Sniffling, Rachel sighed into the phone. "Okay," she replied dejectedly.

CHAPTER TWENTY

Rachel managed to drag her puking-every-five-minutes ass to work in an attempt to get some things done. That ship tipped slightly when she had to run into the bathroom upon arrival to the building and her floor. She decided to inform Kayla of her situation before the office rumor mill did. “He fucking knocked me up!” she broadcasted upon entering Kayla’s office.

“Come again?” a shell-shocked Kayla replied.

“Don’t play coy, you heard me. I’m pregnant, three nausea tormented months to be exact and the icing on the cake, I’m having fucking twins!” she finished plopping into the chair in front of Kayla’s desk watching her open and close her mouth several times.

“Well, I certainly wasn’t expecting THAT to come out of your mouth. Uh, Umm, uh, how are you feeling—doing?” Kayla fumbled.

“I’m feeling like I’ve been invaded and I’m doing horribly. Why didn’t you ever complain about morning sickness or in my revolting case, all day sickness? If I breathe wrong, I’m spewing the contents in my stomach and sometimes there’s nothing in there, but water and they have the NERVE to reject that too. I’m so aggravated, I could spit fire.” Rachel rubbed her hand down her face.

"You know you're exaggerating it's not that bad, and sorry I don't recall having morning sickness," Kayla sheepishly answered.

"Fuck you. Next time, keep that shit to yourself what kind of best friend-sister are you to say that to me? I'm over here having an epic takeover, and you want to tell me how you can't sympathize? I've got work to attempt to do!" Rachel huffed as she got up and headed to the door with Kayla giggling behind her.

Dashawn's day ended earlier than it had in the entire five weeks he'd been in Denver, but he was exhausted. He'd been going non-stop trying to get the firm back in shape and this week, he'd concluded all the meetings necessary as well as provided his boss with a briefing of his final findings. Now, he had to prepare for the daunting task of laying off troublesome employees and shifting their positions to qualified individuals. What he wanted was to go home and check on Rachel in person. Ever since he'd found out she was pregnant, he worried about her and whether she was taking care of herself. Their schedules were mixed up, and it seemed as if she slept every time he called her in the evening. Since it was early, he decided to check on her "Hey Love, you doing okay?" he asked as she answered the phone.

"Right now, I'm despising you. I haven't even gotten into the gist of this pregnancy and I'm cursing you out every hour," she informed him.

"Oh yeah, how come?"

"This all-day sickness your children are giving me is wearing me out. I can't even keep down water. Water! My body needs water, and these little fuckers are rejecting it and everything else," she ranted and whined. "They aren't tolerating shit that I send down and they give it back to me within twenty minutes or less. I think I need an exorcist because this can't be normal. Shit, I might need to go to church or something because I really think God is punishing me!"

Unable to stop himself Dashawn laughed hard. "First, please don't call our children little fuckers, Love. If they can hear you, they'll just make it worse for you. You also don't need an exorcist and church never hurt anybody, although I doubt that God is purposely punishing you."

"I'm glad you think this is so comical! I'm wasting away here. You know I love food and I can't eat anything. My body also doesn't feel like my own. I feel like they have taken over and they're only the size of a pea or something, maybe. Like really, how can something so small cause so much trouble? This is a conspiracy!" Rachel was beside herself.

"Maybe you need to talk with your doctor about this nausea to see if it's normal for you to be sick so much as well as your inability to hold anything including water down. She might have a remedy or solution you can try," he insisted.

"Shit, if her ass isn't suggesting the nearest place to see an exorcist then I call bullshit. Maybe I need to talk to a fortune teller to see if they're even human," she stated.

"Come on now, stop that. There's nothing wrong with my babies. This has to be normal," he provided insightfully.

"Then how about we trade places since all you've done is injected my body with enough fucking sperm to fertilize two gotdamn eggs at one motherfucking time. While we're making the switch, why don't you stay there until you can squeeze both of their asses out of your dick? Just my luck I'll have some big head ass kids that will rip my damn vagina open by the seams…" she trailed off.

"Stop exaggerating Love and call the damn doctor to see if she can give you some relief. Are you showing yet?"

"That's your question while I'm having a whole ass meltdown? Fuck if I know, you know I have a little more cushion in my body…." she stopped talking. "Hold on my line is clicking."

Dashawn sat on hold laughing at Rachel's hysteria wondering how he was going to handle her for the remainder of the pregnancy. It was going to be quite the experience that's for sure he thought as she returned to the line. "Everything all right?"

"Yeah, I gotta go. Kayla is in the driveway, she came over so that we can chat a little more. I dropped the bomb on her at work after getting sick twice upon arrival and then I went to my office where I stayed all day. I'll try to call you once she leaves if the body snatchers don't force me to go to bed. Love you *at the moment*," she finished.

"Damn, isn't that a bitch. You love me at the moment huh? Well, I love your stubborn and mean ass all the damn time, despite how you feel or the things you've said to me tonight. Take care of yourself, Love. Talk to you soon…" Blowing a kiss on the phone, he hung up laughing.

Rachel was lying on her couch glaring at Kayla, but she could only frown for so long as she was holding her god-daughter Maisha on her lap. She was unable to hold her for long, as she was tired and feeling weak from all the throwing up she'd done. "So, Kayla, what's up? I love my god baby and all, but I know you aren't just coming over to come. So get to it, I'm zapped," she snapped.

"Damn, pregnancy has turned you into a mean chick. I'm just waiting for for-ah— I'll get it," she said standing up to answer the door when the doorbell sounded.

Who the fuck is here? A few minutes later, she looked up into the angry face of her cousin Charlene. "Don't say shit, I'm not in the mood today." She returned the glare.

"Too motherfucking bad. How you got two whole people in your body and I'm just now finding out, third hand at that!" Charlene raged.

"Listen, until the man that caused this issue was informed NO ONE could be told," Rachel grumpily spewed out. "So, you can kiss my ass right now. I've been sick for weeks, and I haven't felt like breathing, let alone having friendly ass conversations. Besides, it looks like you've been informed now so get over it!"

"You lucky your ass laying on that couch looking like you're two seconds from being an extra on Night of the Living Dead or I'd kick your ass, pregnant or not," Charlene promised.

"Yeah and you lucky I love your ass, or I'd allow you to become acquainted with my pregnancy condition. Now what the fuck is this meeting about?" she ranted.

"You know we need to go ahead and call the conference line and give our other sisters the 411," Kayla informed her.

"The only thing that I know is that in six months, my pussy is gonna part just as wide as the Red Sea did for Moses!" Rachel huffed.

"Maybe, maybe not, you could be me and have a cesarean," Kayla taunted.

"So, just because your ass can now pick up the impending weather by the response in your back, doesn't mean I want or need to join you. I'm not interested in being cut open. That's just bullshit!" Rachel yelled causing Maisha to whimper slightly. "Sorry pumpkin."

"Keep it down before you scare this sweet baby with your loud mouth and hysterics," Charlene stated smiling at the baby.

"Whatever, I barely register normal behavior. Is it too early for baby brain? These *little terrors* have already made their presence known," she ranted.

"Hmmph, sounds to me like they're acting like their momma and I for one… LOVE it!" Charlene hooted.

"Truthfully, so do I. You do remember what you told Maisha when she was born, don't you? Just wait for it, payback is a Bitch soaked in gasoline drawers!" Kayla laughed.

Rachel laid on the couch staring at her cousin and one of her best friends unable to think of anything to fire back with. These babies were indeed torturing her. *Dashawn's ass better buckle up cause this ride is going to be bumpy as hell for him.* "Call the damn conference line before I put all your asses out of my house."

"Gladly," Kayla and Charlene said as Charlene hit the number programmed in her cell phone.

"Hey Sisters, Jocelyn reporting in."

"Sup girls, Caressa here."

"Present on the line, it's Reia."

"Crisis line, Monica present. What's today's incident of discussion?"

"What it do ladies? This is Charlene. Kayla and I are over Rachel's house. Oh yeah, Maisha is present too," she finished as Maisha cooed hearing all of her auntie's voices.

"Oh Lawd, what's the emergency this time?" Caressa probed.

"Damn Rachel, whatchu done did now?" Reia teased.

"Ok, before we prolong this shit any longer here it is… I'm three months pregnant with twins and I'm not sure they're human but yeah, that's the emergency today," Rachel informed the group.

"It's about time! I mean uh, shit I got nothing other than that…" Jocelyn stopped on a snicker.

"Well, welcome to the "mommy club" FINALLY!" Reia taunted.

"Anybody else wants to break out a bottle of wine and take it to the head?" Caressa inquired.

"Are y'all fucking kidding me right now?" Rachel laughed as the women broke out into hysterical giggles.

Monica chimed in, "Look I know I'm the newbie to this group and I don't have any children or a man yet, but anyway, I've noticed that you have corrupted my niece, so I'm excited to see these women turn the tables back on you. Oh, and double the trouble, double the fun with twins!"

"This shit is gonna be fun to watch," Charlene stated. "If you could see the death glare she be giving this phone right now though. You all might want to be on high alert. She looks like her head might spin around any second. Come on cousin, it's not that deep."

"First, these little terrorizers turn my body into their incubator and now, my circle of family has turned their backs on me for spite and revenge. This is some straight up bullshit," Rachel said sadly, fighting the tears that she wasn't trying to release.

"Um, is she over there about to cry? What the hell is going on right now?" Jocelyn asked.

"Oh yeah, she's extra emotional and sick," Kayla informed them. "She seems to be fighting all day morning sickness. So who knows how she'll respond to anything."

Rachel couldn't do anything but flick them off as she started crying, "I-I, h-have n-nothing to say to any of you," she sobbed then hiccupped then cupped her mouth as she jumped up and ran to the nearest bathroom.

"Yeah, this is gonna be an interesting time for all of us," Charlene said watching her cousin run off.

Rachel returned from the bathroom a short while later looking worn out and tired as she sat down on the couch and five minutes later, she was out like a light. She didn't hear the jokes turn to concern because she was sleeping hard. Somewhere in the recesses of her mind, she still cussed them out and talked to her unborn children. Stop torturing Mommy, you little terrors.

Dashawn exited the plane the following Friday night with one destination in mind—Rachel. As he grabbed his luggage, he picked up his car from long-term parking and made a B-line for her house. Ever since he found out she was pregnant, his panic and protective instincts went to another level. Twenty minutes at ticket inducing speeds, he pulled into her driveway and noted how dark the house was which brought back unpleasant memories of a similar scene not long ago.

Exiting the car, he jogged to the door and rung the bell as his keys to her house were at home.

A short time later, a sleep-ridden yet pissed off Rachel opened the door.

"Aren't you a sight for my tired eyes." He leaned in kissing her.

"Yeah, yeah, you woke me up and I was sleeping well. These little terrors have been draining me since their existence was confirmed," she grumbled closing the door then headed back to her bed.

"Will you stop calling my babies names. How're you doing?" he asked with a serious look of concern.

"Still puking my guts out but now, I'm able to handle crackers and ginger ale. I'm hungry, tired, and pissed off. How are you?" she asked sarcastically.

"Since I'm standing in front of you, better." He smirked at the look on her face.

"Yep, that may change in a little while when you've seen me spew liquid from my mouth and nostrils," she said climbing into her bed.

"Not likely after all you're carrying my babies," he boasted then ducked when a pillow came flying his way.

"Now, is not a good time to remind me, asshole."

"Nice way to welcome your man home from being away six weeks. Let me go wash this travel off me. I'll be back." He smirked and headed to her bathroom. He found his belongings in the same place they'd been the last time he stayed over. *May need to bring more things over here.* After a quick shower, Dashawn toweled off and walked back into the bedroom to find Rachel sound asleep hugging a pillow. *Looks like an angel, until she wakes up that is.* Sliding in the bed without clothes, he removed her from the pillow and whispering as he positioned her under his arm, "No need to hug this pillow, I'll provide you all the comfort you need." For the first time in six weeks, Dashawn felt at peace as he settled in, drifting off a few minutes later.

CHAPTER TWENTY-ONE

Time is flying, seven months already. Rachel and Dashawn were sitting in the waiting room at her OB's office. Her pregnancy was progressing nicely, and she'd finally been able to overcome her morning sickness much to both of their delights. Rubbing her belly, she smiled at Dashawn. "So what do you think we're having? I'm still thinking they're alien," she joked.

"When they keep you up all night, remember that they are getting back at you," he said leaning over to give her a quick peck just as the nurse called her name. "Showtime," he happily expressed.

Rachel waddled to the nurse, greeting her as they made their way to the exam room, "Hey Claudia, do you think we'll be able to see them this time?" she asked the nurse.

"Hard to say. Hopefully, they'll cooperate this morning," Claudia replied.

Rachel got on the exam table with the assistance of Dashawn and lifted her shirt. "Be nice in there, your daddy wants to know who's causing his woman so much trouble," she told her stomach.

Laughing, Claudia shook her head. "Dr. Montgomery will be in momentarily."

Dashawn looked at Rachel with so much pride and love on his face. "Oh, so you think I have influence with them, huh?"

"Yup, these *little terrors* respond to you better than me, and I'm their human sacrifice."

"Probably, because you call them *little terrors,*" he said as the doctor entered the room.

"Good morning you two. How are things going? Are you feeling ok, mommy? You just entered your seventh month. Let's take a look at how things are going and maybe we'll be able to see the sex. They seem to fight that task though," the doctor finished squirting the ultrasound goo on her stomach and turning on the machine.

"Well, if their momma would play nice, maybe they would too. They're just as stubborn as her ass is," Dashawn teased.

"Oh, shut up, they already got your sappy ass wrapped around their fingers," Rachel said watching the monitor.

"Good strong heartbeat for baby A, now let me look at baby B and then we'll see if they'll move so we can see their parts. Good strong heartbeat for baby B as well. Come on sweeties, shift positions, so we can see who's going to give mommy and daddy a run for their money," Dr. Montgomery teased. Swirling the wand around then pausing and swirling a little more then pressing down lightly, the doctor spoke, "These babies are stubborn, who's personality are they displaying? They're not budging."

"Their mother's." Dashawn smirked.

"Whatever." Rachel rolled her eyes. "Let me see if I can get them to move. Come on *little terrors*, play nice I need to know who to prepare for," she told her stomach as she moved one side of her belly and then the other.

"Uh, they don't seem to like that name," Dr. Montgomery booed watching as the babies moved with one baby's arms flailing and the other's leg kicking out against the wand. "But I think we might have gotten them mad enough for me to see, looks like you might have one of each. Congratulations, although you might need to give them better names," the doctor said as she cleaned Rachel up having made a quick print of the ultrasound.

"When they stop torturing me, I'll think about it," Rachel stubbornly replied rubbing her protruding belly with a small smile on her face. "So, Mr. Sanders are you happy with the sexes?" She peered at him.

"Regardless of their sex, I'm quite happy," he proudly stated.

"Alright you two, I'll see you soon. Set up your next appointment with the receptionist and Rachel… take it easy we want those babies in there as long as possible," Dr. Montgomery provided then walked out of the room.

Dashawn helped Rachel get into his car and felt a sense of overwhelming excitement hit him. He couldn't be happier to know that he was just a couple of months away from holding not one but two babies in his arms. He felt elated to hear that he was getting a boy and a girl right out of the gate. His life would only get better when he and Rachel were married, and they all were Sanders because he definitely, wasn't allowing her to name them Spencer or hyphenate the names.

"What's with that goofy smirk you're wearing?" Rachel snapped cutting into his musings.

"Just really happy is all, although I'd be happier if we were married. How about we get married before the babies are born?" he posed.

"You must have inhaled some of the gunk that Dr. Montgomery rubbed on my stomach. Are you crazy? Not only do you knock me up after a sexual break, give me twins and NOW you want me to waddle my big ass down an aisle for us to get married. Hell, to the fucking no. I bet that's what we won't be doing. Shit, just my luck my big ass would go into labor right as the vows got good. Fuck that, you'll have to wait and be okay with your children being born bastards," she ranted.

Dashawn just stared at her for a minute as if she had two heads. "So I take it you don't want to marry me," he spoke finally.

"Not if it requires me to put on some fat suit, fuck that. Why are you looking at me like that?" she spat.

"Just wondering if you or the babies are talking right now. You realize you've cussed me out constantly since you found out you were pregnant as if you hate my guts or something. You haven't even let me touch you," he informed her.

"Oh buddy, your touching me is what's causing me to look like the Goodyear blimp right now. Get out of your damn feelings. I'll love you again when this is over," she fired back.

Rachel rolled her eyes as she remembered how Dashawn practically carried her up to her floor and in her office. He acted like she was made of glass or something and it was irritating her to no end. Her assistant came in her office just as she plopped down in her chair. "What's up Megan?"

"Honey, every time that man of yours gives us the rarity of his presence, there's buzzing around for here for an hour afterward. These thirst buckets wish they could be you right now, boss lady."

"If they want to deal with my swollen ankles, constant indigestion, and the rest of the pregnancy woes, then sure, have at it. But what they asses will never get is my damn man. Tell those bitches to find they own man to drool over, that six feet one inch of chocolate goodness belongs to me," she replied flashing her ring.

"Believe me, I know. That man doesn't look anywhere but wherever your mean ass is," her assistant commented.

"Uh, did you forget that I'm responsible for your pay increases around here? Did you just call me mean to my face?" She raised her eyes.

"No offense boss… but damn, you are a pregnant force to be reckoned with. The rumor mill doesn't fail to spread the word of keeping a wide berth around you these days."

"Wide berth are you motherfuckers calling me fat?" Rachel hollered.

"Not at all." Megan dropped her head.

"I'll whoop somebody's ass up in here, pregnant or not," she continued yelling, noting Kayla walking towards her office.

"You want to tell me why I can hear you screaming down the hall Rachel? What's going on that you need to be hollering? Don't forget my nieces or nephews don't like stress. What are we having anyway?" Kayla asked walking into her office as Megan dashed out closing the door.

"Why is there a plural behind each sex? I also don't care if the *little terrors* don't like stress as much as they keep me up during the night. *THEY* are stress inducers themselves." She shrugged.

"Do I need to call Dashawn on your ass? Calm down," Kayla demanded.

"Oh, please call his ass, I beg you to call him," she said holding her phone out.

"Girl, you're a mess." Kayla shook her head. "Are you gonna tell me what you're having?

"How about we do the conference line cause I'm not about to repeat myself multiple times till everybody knows. Let me see if Dashawn wants to do it tonight, we need to tell our parents anyway. I'll call him now, hold tight."

Dashawn picked up the phone after a few rings "Hey Love, I just left you not long ago. Is everything good?" he quizzically inquired.

"Stop worrying babe, we still have two months to go and I've told the *little terrors* to stay in there as long as they want. Anyway, Kayla's here and wants to know the sex, so I was wondering if you wanted to call our parents over to the house today and we can tell them and the out of town girls at one time. What do you think?"

"Sounds like a good idea. I'll pick up dinner for everyone and we can have an impromptu dinner party. I'll call my mom. Is that all you wanted?"

"I like that idea babe, I'll call my dad, and yep, that's all I needed. Are you picking me up or sending an Uber?"

"Hell no, I'm not sending an Uber. I'll be there to get you!" Dashawn ranted.

"Roger that, talk to you later," she ended the calling laughing.

"Uh, why did he get all possessive about Uber, did I miss something?" Kayla giggled.

"Girl, he's been bringing me to work for a couple of weeks now, he thinks I'm too big to be behind the wheel." She looked down at her very round belly smirking.

"Yeah, I can see that your stomach seems to get bigger by the minute Sis. Wow, my stomach looked like a watermelon compared to what you're carrying around. No wonder your ass is so mean all the damn time," she finished.

"Here we go with this mean shit. I'm not mean. I'm misguided," she bragged.

"Let's take a poll around the office and see who wins or let's ask Dashawn! I bet his ass has been scared to sleep around you. Mean ass!" She laughed.

"Whatever," Rachel replied dialing her father's number. "Hey Dad, we're doing a gender reveal at my house this evening, can you come?" she asked when her father picked up.

"Sure can, what time should I come Chelly?" Lee asked.

"Come about six because we're providing dinner as well," she cheerily stated.

"Okay, see you at six. Oh, do I need to bring anything?"

"Just yourself dad, see you at six," she told him then disconnected the call. Looking at Kayla she said, "You don't forget to bring my Pumpkin, oh and Myles can come too." She snickered.

"They were coming. Anyway, this is a family event. I'll see you at six, don't work too hard," Kayla joked heading towards the door.

"Yes, ma'am *boss* lady," she taunted.

"Stop!" Kayla jested leaving the office.

Around four-thirty, Dashawn arrived at her door.

"Can you give me a few minutes to wrap this up?" she requested quickly glancing in his direction.

"No problem, but don't forget that we need to be at the house and ready to receive our guests before they arrive at six."

"I know. I just need to get this formula to return the correct result and I've been fighting with it for a little while now," she said aggravated.

"Good thing I got off early and went to the house to set up as well as grab the food. You have a little bit of time but not a ton of time," he informed her.

"Your wonderful babe, thank you," she replied without looking up from her computer to see his happy face from her compliment.

CHAPTER TWENTY-TWO

Promptly at six o'clock, Dashawn's mom and stepdad arrived followed by Rachel's dad, Lee, then Kayla, Myles, and Maisha. Bringing up the rear was Charlene along with her Aunt Mae.

"Welcome everyone," Dashawn greeted.

"Hi, guys. Thanks for joining us," Rachel said when they all walked into the dining room.

"Let's get this party popping. Hey, Uncle Lee," Charlene spoke hugging Rachel's dad.

"Hey Char, I'm not your uncle you trying to get me in trouble, huh?" Lee greeted back.

"In trouble with who Uncle Lee? I'm a grown ass woman and can say whatever I want," Charlene said.

Aunt Mae grinned. "My family holds no grudges against you, Lee. My daughter is also like your daughter so whether they did or not, she'd move by her own drumbeat."

"Now, that we got that out of the way, how about we eat?" Rachel expressed rubbing her enormous belly.

"Your house, your rules," everyone murmured.

"So, I wasn't sure what we'd be in the mood for, so I went to City Barbeque and got a few things. If this isn't to your satisfaction Rachel, I'll gladly go on a food run once our guests leave," Dashawn told the group and Rachel.

"Aw, that's so sweet," Kayla whimpered.

"Isn't it though, she got your ass over here living out the lyrics to *Cater to You* Rachel, you're my Shero girl." Charlene fake wiped her eyes causing everyone to laugh.

"I'm sorry Mr. and Mrs. Tate, my crazy cousin Charlene doesn't mean any harm, but she's the impromptu entertainment for tonight," Rachel kidded.

"Sweetie, you don't have to apologize or anything we're family which means we'll get along just fine." Mrs. Tate smirked.

"Honey, hush. I like you!" Charlene yelled causing the room to explode with laughter.

"Dig in everyone then we can get to the good stuff," Dashawn stated.

Rachel stood in the front of the living room a short while later with Dashawn standing beside her, with one hand on her back and the other on her stomach. "The gang's all here right, Jocelyn, Reia, Caressa, you there?" she asked into her cell phone.

"We're here Sis, and ready to hear the good news," Jocelyn replied.

"Well, we went for our first ultrasound at four months, and the little terrors wouldn't cooperate for us, so we had no idea what they were. Dashawn keeps promising me that they're human, but my jury is still out."

"Did she just call those babies, little terrors?" Aunt Mae chimed in.

"Yes, ma'am," Dashawn said hanging his head. "I've been trying to get her out of it, but she hasn't shifted to a more suitable nickname or something for them yet."

"Oh Lord, Rachel please tell me you're not planning on naming those babies Terror One and Terror Two?" Charlene laughed.

Mrs. Tate asked while looking panicked, "Honey hush. She wouldn't. Dashawn you're not gonna let her do that to our babies are you?"

"No Ma, we aren't naming them that. Rachel and I will give them appropriate names. I promise," he replied to his mother who let out a deep breath of relief.

"Oh God, Chelly. You aren't serious with those names, right?" Lee asked.

Rachel rolled her eyes. "Uh, you guys are sidetracked unnecessarily. I promise we'll name them appropriately just as Dashawn stated. Now can we get back to business? As I was stating since they wouldn't cooperate and there's two of them, my doctor was kind enough to perform another ultrasound today. Drum roll please?"

"Blrrrrr…." Dashawn and Myles mocked a drum roll.

"Thanks, guys. In about two months, we're going to be welcoming a boy and a girl to the Sanders family." Rachel smiled as everyone clapped and hooted.

"We're happy that we'll be having one of each or at least I am cause I'm not sure if Rachel will allow us to experience this again," Dashawn joked.

"Aw, that'll pass as soon as these two are born." His mother shrugged it off.

"Yep, I recall saying the same thing to Carter, and then I proceeded to have another one," Reia spoke into the phone.

"We'll see how this goes before we start talking about future children, m'kay?" Rachel deadpanned.

"Ok, so I know you just found out but have y'all thought of names? We could turn this into a naming session," Charlene offered.

"We'll discuss it between Dashawn and me first, and you all will find out the names on the day we deliver," Rachel told them.

"Booo…" all the girls chimed in over the speaker phone.

Dashawn followed his parents to their car. "So how happy are you two? Boy and girl, out the gate?" he bragged.

"Very happy, although I'm wondering why your future wife calls my first grandchildren *little terrors*," his stepdad pondered.

"Don't be offended, James. I doubt that she means anything about it," Dashawn defended.

"Neither do I truthfully," his mother also defended. "I've been pregnant before and believe me when hormones are raging, you could be called anything but a child of God. She's also carrying two, so that's double trouble. They must be taking her through some changes."

"That's exactly it." Dashawn nodded. "She spent months with all day sickness, and they wouldn't let her eat or drink. Ever since then she's adopted that nickname. I personally hate it, but do you know how she responded one time when I asked her to stop? She told me to switch places with her and especially, come delivery day squeeze two big head ass babies out of my penis. The thought alone made me reach for said penis!" He laughed at the horrified look on his step father's face.

"Oh man, can't say I blame you. She's definitely gonna make parenting with her and marriage a ball of fun," James teased.

"I know, and it's why I love her stubborn ass. She compliments my world and personality very well. I can't wait to marry her mean ass," he stated proudly.

"When is the wedding anyway?" his mother inquired.

"Hopefully after the babies are born, she checked my ass about that too, not too long ago. I'm just trying to keep her healthy and happy right now."

"Smart man," his mother and James added wrapping up the conversation.

A few weeks later, Rachel was having lunch with Monica who'd been out of town during the impromptu gender reveal. She felt she was being watched when she looked up and saw a woman with a strong resemblance to her, staring at her.

Monica noting Rachel's face stopped talking and looked up. "Do you know that woman Rachel? Why is she just staring at you?"

Rachel was unable to respond, her gut was telling her who she was, but she couldn't confirm it. As the woman made her way slowly over, she remembered the conversation she had with her dad about her siblings as well as the one they had during a lunch they had a couple of weeks after her mother passed.

…"Chelly, I know you're going through a lot right now, and I won't push, so let me know when you're ready to meet your brother and sister."

"I'm not sure that I'm really up to meet them," she soberly responded. "I mean, I've been going all this time without them in my life I'm not sure what any of us would get out of meeting. Either they'll wind up resenting me, or I'll wind up resenting them for having you. I spent my whole childhood wishing you could be a part of my life and they got that experience. I'm not sure that wouldn't make me resentful. I'm sorry, but I just don't think it's a good idea. I want to build a relationship with just you."

"I respect your decision and if you ever change your mind let me know. You have made excellent points, and I'm not sure that any of us thought of you or your feelings about that. I appreciate your being honest with me. Now, how often does a man get to see his daughter?" Lee probed.

"As often as time allows Dad. I'm enjoying your company today. After losing Mom, it's been hard, but the void is a little bearable knowing you're a phone call away. It's weird that I miss her so much when she was

so reckless in my life, but even in her lack of parenting she was still my parent, you know?" she thoughtfully provided.

"I know, and I'm sorry that I wasn't around and that you're feeling her death in so many ways. Nobody can tell you how to feel, so you do what's best for Rachel in this. Remember that there are people around you who will love you through it and you're not alone."...

Rachel gasped as she realized the woman was directly in front of her as she remembered the last words her father said before their lunch ended. "Uh, do I know you?" she asked the woman.

"We don't technically know each other, but we know *of* each other. Although you have never seen me, I've seen pictures of you. My name is Nisha Spencer, and I'm your sister."

Rachel just sat there unconsciously rubbing her belly unsure of what to say. "Uh, hi," she hesitantly responded feeling cornered.

"Listen, I know Dad said you weren't ready for a family reunion so to speak but I couldn't just ignore you. I've been anxious to meet you for a long time. I was also sorry to hear about the passing of your Mom," she sheepishly said.

"Thanks for coming over. I'll let Dad know we saw each other," Rachel dismissed her giving Monica a gesture. "If you'll excuse me I need to go to the bathroom," she carefully stood and began walking away.

But her sister wasn't interested in being brushed off. "Are you kidding me right now? You're walking away just like that?" She caught her by the arm stopping her retreat.

"I suggest you let go of my arm or I'll forget that we have a smidgen of the same blood running through our veins," Rachel angrily replied.

Monica rushed over. "Listen chick, you need to back the fuck off." She stepped closer to Rachel in a defensive posture.

"Bitch, who do you think you are? I'll beat your ass for just talking to me and interfering in business that's not yours." Nisha growled.

"Oh, it's my business when you decided to stay instead of walking away with your dignity intact," Monica ranted. "Have you failed to see the *pregnant* sister you're standing in front of?"

Rachel hadn't forgotten her pregnancy as her stomach was tightening the angrier she became. "Look, bitch, you need to move your ass anywhere but in front of me," she stated, as her voice grew tighter and more forceful.

"Make me!" Her sister moved closer and almost bumping her stomach.

Looking over at Monica, Rachel sneered. "This Bitch would do this shit NOW when beating her ass would be wrong in my condition." Turning to face her sister again she stated, "This is EXACTLY why I will never fuck with you. We'll meet again when I deliver my babies because an ass-whooping is what you just cashed a check for. Now BACK. THE. FUCK. UP. OUT. OF. MY. FACE. BEFORE. I. LET. YOU. CASH. IT. NOW. The next time we see each other, I promise you revenge.

Until then Bitch!" She charged away pissed that she couldn't handle her business now.

Monica caught up with Rachel. "Are you okay?"

Rachel stomped into the bathroom with the door slamming against the wall with the force of her anger. "HELL no, I want to fight. How dare she come for me right now? These *little terrors* just saved her life, but I promise you that they won't be her saving grace for long!" She went into the nearest stall. When she sat down to relieve herself, she felt her stomach tighten and release repeatedly. "Shit!" she retorted now feeling the pain. "Uh, Monica, you might want to call Dashawn and tell him to meet us at the hospital," she breathed out heavily as the pain increased.

"Damn it! Where's your phone?" Monica yelled.

"Right here," she replied waddling slowly out of the stall toward the sink where she gripped it hard. "It's too early little terrors… you're not ready. I'm sorry for getting worked up," she talked to the babies. "Dashawn is going to lose his shit.

Dashawn was beyond livid. He'd gotten a call from a frazzled Monica, telling him that she was taking Rachel to the hospital. At first, he panicked then when he found out why she was on her way to the hospital, he was pissed off. Dialing Rachel's father's number, he tried to contain his anger, "Sup Lee, do you know that your daughter caused my fucking fiancé to begin having contractions?

If something happens to her or my kids, heads will be rolled the fuck off!" he growled.

"What?" Lee shockingly asked.

"It appears that Rachel and Monica were having lunch and were approached and later ambushed by your other daughter. Rachel dismissed her from what Monica told me, and it caused her to become childish. Instead of walking away noting Rachel's condition, she pushed and even grabbed her by her arm. Hell, she bumped her body up against Rachel! She's pregnant with twins who don't do well with stress, so they're responding to that. I'm heading to the hospital now."

"Jesus, Christ!" Lee yelled when he stopped talking. "Son of a bitch, let me get to the bottom of this shit. I told Nisha that Rachel wasn't ready and she had to try and force her hand any damn way. I'm sorry, please keep me posted. Fuck, I was making headway, now she'll probably stop our relationship…" Lee sighed.

"Truthfully, I don't give two fucks about your dilemma. Just wanted you to know the situation and consequences if anything happens to MY family." He punched the end button. Pulling into the garage of the hospital, he quickly found a place to park and hurried into labor and delivery. "I'm looking for Rachel Spencer?" he heavily panted to the desk clerk.

"Down the hall on the left, room 328," she told him.

Walking into the room a few minutes later he noted the chaos in the room and Rachel was visibly upset. "Oh God, what's wrong?" he asked while rushing to Rachel's side.

"Had I known this, I would have just beat her ass!" Rachel cried.

Monica started laughing.

"What? Can someone please tell me what's going on? Is there something wrong with the babies?"

"Calm down Dashawn and prepare yourself cause the *little terrors* are coming early," Rachel told him wiping her eyes.

"It's too early, what do you mean? Dr. Montgomery?"

The doctor nodded. "Dashawn, the stress Rachel experienced earlier caused her to go into pre-term labor, while it's not uncommon for twins I was hoping they'd stay inside longer. I've started meds to assist with the development of their lungs and trying to stop her contractions, but they seem pretty upset and resistant in there," she concluded rubbing Rachel's belly as it tightened.

Dashawn watched Rachel grimace tightly. "Love, you all right?" he questioned.

"Do I look like I'm all right? I'm in pain, unprepared for labor, no mother to help me through it, no fucking father thanks to his bitch ass oldest daughter. On top of that, you're looking like you're gonna fall at any moment. Hell-shit- motherfucker-oh my gawd!" she finished as the next contraction hit her stronger than the previous.

"What can I do Love?" he asked unsure of her reply.

"Get me someone here that won't crumble if I call them names, cry, and act a gotdamn fool. Call the girls to let them know what's going on. Call Charlene first though I don't want her crazy ass on no bullshit when she gets here. Ooh, and please call your mom, tell her I need her to be my parental focal point," she panted heavily.

Looking at Dr. Montgomery, he asked, "Can she have drugs? I don't imagine she wants to do this without them…" He peeked at Rachel.

"Sure, let me check her, and then we'll work on getting her some relief now that we know that these babies insist on coming out of there," Dr. Montgomery stated as she slipped on gloves. "Ah, yep they're definitely coming, you're already six centimeters dilated. Let's get the anesthesiologist in here while we have the time. They get antsy and won't perform it if you go too much further," she finished leaving the room.

"Looks like its show time folks," Dashawn said leaning down to kiss Rachel as she rolled her eyes.

CHAPTER TWENTY-THREE

"Oh my God, I'm so sorry. I promise I won't fuck—I mean have sex with Dashawn again! Please make it stop hurting. Oh God, oh God!" Rachel whined.

"No sex? Uh, y'all need to increase her meds because she's hallucinating or something," Dashawn responded holding her hand.

"Shut up you asshole, my damn body, my damn pussy, your ass fucking did this shit to me. Oh God, this fucking hurts!" she cried.

"I'm sorry baby but push, and it'll get easier," he told her.

"How about you push two motherfucking babies out of your dick and then we talk about how it'll get easier!" she yelled.

"Rachel, you've got to quit screaming and concentrate on pushing," Dr. Montgomery said in a calm voice as if she was talking to a child. "Screaming only makes it worse. Now focus and let's deliver these babies."

Looking at Mrs. Tate on her other side, Rachel attempted a smile as she noted her calm nod "Okay, okay," she said bearing down and pushing.

"GOTDAMN, IS THAT A HEAD?" Dashawn yelled.

Nobody answered him as they continued coaching Rachel on pushing, then she felt a release and popping sound. Seconds later, she heard the first cries of her firstborn.

"Baby A is out, and it's a boy. Congratulations mom and dad!" Dr. Montgomery smiled holding the baby up and then passing him off to the awaiting nurse.

"Fuck!" Rachel screamed out.

"Looks like baby B is ready to join her brother. Push Rachel."

Rachel gripped Dashawn's hand to the point of pain as he grimaced, "Suck it up motherfucker this is your fault!" she yelled.

Moments later, Dr. Montgomery yelled, "Don't push, Rachel. Stop pushing. Stop!" she was saying.

"What? I can't hold it!" she said continuing to push then she screamed as she ripped. "Oww," she cried as the baby came out crying.

"Uh, here's Baby B. Congratulations guys, looks like the ultrasound was incorrect you have another son," Dr. Montgomery told them shaking her head holding the baby up but again, passed him off to another nurse. "Hold tight Rachel. I'll have to sew you up, you're ripped from stem to sternum down here."

Dashawn walked away from Rachel then turned to see the tear and his timing was terrible as the afterbirth came at that moment. "What the fuck is that?" he dazedly asked, and then he hit the floor.

A little while later, Rachel laid in the hospital bed, exhausted from the painful delivery she'd experienced just about an hour earlier. It hurt like a mother, despite the epidural she had since she was delivering two babies. She couldn't believe how things turned out or the fact that Dashawn's big ass hit the floor after the babies were delivered. *I did all the damn work, and he passes out? Bullshit.* Looking at him lying beside her now, she hoped that he was okay. They'd had a time, but she loved him more than she ever thought she could or would for that matter.

"Can you believe we have two SONS?" Dashawn exclaimed.

"No, and that second *little terror* had to make a grand entrance by tearing me in two. His little ass isn't big enough to have caused me to rip, but he was demanding his escape and wouldn't let up until he got out. I couldn't stop fucking pushing, and now I'll be sitting in sitz baths and on a donut for a little while. This is bullshit," she ranted and then smirked. For the first time since finding out about her pregnancy, she was happy. *It's been a hell of a pregnancy.*

"I know but can we not tell anybody that I passed out?" Dashawn requested.

"Did you forget that your mother and Monica were here? I'm pretty sure Monica told the gang as soon as she informed them of the baby's arrival." Rachel laughed.

"Shit, I'm never living this down with the other dads," he replied hanging his head in shame.

"At all…" Rachel patted his head as she continued laughing.

Dashawn was lying next to Rachel who'd dozed off causing her to snuggle up to him, and before he knew it, he fell asleep too. That is until he heard a nurse calling them causing him to wake up first. "Yeah, yeah?" he replied drowsily.

"I'm sorry to bother you Mr. Sanders, but I need to make you both aware of something. Can you wake Ms. Spencer?" the nurse wavered.

Dashawn tapped Rachel gently. "Love, the nurse is here and needs to tell us something."

Rachel woke slowly looking at him and then the nurse. "I'm sorry, I'm pooped. Is there something wrong?" she paused looking at the nurse.

"Uh, yes. One of your sons is having some trouble breathing so we had to hook him up to oxygen. His reaction caused your other son to become unstable, so we had to hook him up to oxygen as well."

"Are you kidding me? Now, they're playing off each other. Lawd, these babies are going to be the death of me. Can we see them? My only view was them dangling for a second in the air after they were born…" Rachel sighed.

"Sure, Ms. Spencer are you able to walk?" the nurse asked.

"I believe I will be all right. If not, Dashawn will be there to help me maneuver," Rachel said becoming worried about her children who didn't even have names yet. "We haven't even named them or seen them properly, and they're on oxygen" she began weeping silently.

"They're going to be fine Love. Let's go check on them and give them words of encouragement. We can also name them when we see them," Dashawn said taking her hand as he helped her out of bed and toward the door.

Rachel slowly walked into the NICU uncertain of what would await them when they got to the cribs. “Are they separated?” she asked the nurse that stood to the side.

“Yes, they are separate,” the nurse answered.

“How are they doing, now that the oxygen is breathing for them?” a worried Dashawn questioned.

“They’re holding their own,” the nurse stated. “Baby B was pulling pretty hard after we got him here, so we felt that he’d do better if we gave him some help.”

“Uh, are we able to hold them?” Rachel reluctantly asked.

“Not yet, we need them to become stable before we move them.”

Rachel overcome with emotions that were spiraling started crying. “I don’t understand any of this. Nobody told me that there was a problem and I was just waiting for them to be brought to their dad and me. Now, I’m watching a machine breathe for them.”

Dashawn wrapped his arms around her hugging her to him. “I know but you’re getting worked up won’t help them. They’re going to be fine. Can we have a chair to sit with them for a little while?” he asked the nurse.

“Of course, you can. Let me grab a couple for you.”

“So, have you considered some names for our children? I’m thinking *little terrors* or baby A and B won’t work,” Dashawn proposed.

"I've been doing some thinking and I have some first names picked out if you can come up with their middle names?" she posed.

"No problem." Dashawn nodded. "Write them down, and we'll present them when we introduce them to our family."

The nurse then came back and set the chairs up. "The boys are doing okay, all things considered. I know that they look anything but with the tubes hooked up and all, but we're confident that they'll be just fine," the nurse told them as she stood in front of Aiden's crib.

"How can you honestly say that they're going to be okay? My babies are on a breathing machine!" Rachel yelled on a broken sob.

"Calm down Rachel, it's not her fault, and she's just trying to keep things positive and in perspective. Besides, if that woman hadn't worked you up in the first place, we might not even be here." Dashawn snarled.

"Ms. Spencer, I'm sorry I didn't mean to make you upset and I meant nothing by my statement. Just wanted to give you some reassurance that your babies will be fine…" she stopped as alarms began to sound from Jayden's crib.

"Oh God, what's going on?" a panic-stricken Rachel inquired.

"Nurse? What's wrong with our son?" Dashawn nervously asked as other nurses, as they and a doctor began to swarm the incubator.

Ten days later, Rachel sat on the couch feeding one of the babies as Dashawn fed the other, it had been a crazy rollercoaster ride, but she was happy with the end result. “I’m glad that I decided against breastfeeding with these greedy little terrors,” she said watching the baby suck hard on the nipple.

“I would have rather you breastfed them. They say breast is best.” Dashawn grinned at her.

“Ok, the next time I’ll let you breastfeed and I’ll change diapers,” she taunted.

“The day I produce milk will be the day that the world comes tumbling to a close,” he told her as he smiled.

“My thoughts exactly. How the hell do you think I could produce enough milk for two babies? Good thing we didn’t find out, besides that would have been the end of your ability to cherish my nipples. You *and* the babies couldn’t suck on them.”

The doorbell rang as the babies finished their bottles. “Perfect timing boys,” Dashawn said standing with the baby and heading to the door. “Welcome everyone, how did you all manage to get here at the same time?” he greeted the group of people waiting on the porch.

“Congratulations, Humpty Dumpty!” Charlene taunted causing the group to laugh at his expense.

“Don’t make me leave your ass on this porch Char,” he grumpily replied.

“Aw, Son don’t be mad at her cause you hit the floor like a ton of bricks. I’ve never seen anybody drop so fast,” his mother joined in the teasing.

"Seriously, Ma? Not you too?" He shook his head.

"Let us in this house and hand me that baby!" She walked to him and took the baby out of his arms.

"Are y'all going to continue congregating at the door or are you coming in here?" Rachel yelled from the living room.

A few short minutes later, everyone was gathered in the living room making googly eyes at the babies.

"So, I'm guessing we should get started since you're all here. I'm so glad that you made it, Caressa, Jocelyn, and Reia. I also want to begin by saying thank you to Monica for not only having my back, but also by staying in the delivery room with me. I truly appreciate it," Rachel choked out.

"Damn, I thought her sappy ass would have gotten better after the babies came?" Reia ribbed.

"I know! I'm not used to her being a bag of water. It's a little unsettling cause she's too damn mean for sappy," Caressa wearily provided.

"Don't start this shit," Rachel joshed.

"And just like that, her mean and hateful comes barreling back to the front girls," Jocelyn smartly stated. "Don't worry she's still in there!"

"Anyway, we're glad you're here, so we can properly introduce you to our sons. It's been quite the experience for us over the past couple of weeks. But I think we're holding up just fine." Rachel winked at Dashawn.

"Yes, we are Love. We've decided on the names of our boys, being held by mom is Baby A as he was referred to in the womb was born at five pounds twelve ounces and nineteen inches long. His name is Aiden Daniel Sanders. Being held by Rachel because they have a special bond is Baby B who came out weighing six pounds one ounce and twenty inches long of torturous fun. His name is Jayden Dwayne Sanders. You are welcome to hold both babies but please wash your hands first and good luck getting Jayden away from his momma. He's already a momma's boy and barely lets me hold him," he concluded with the most prominent and broadest smile on his face.

"I think since he ripped me open, I've established that we should be on good terms." Rachel smirked as she kissed little Jayden.

"Well, at least you've named them something other than *little terrors,*" Monica provided on a contagious laugh as the group laughed hysterically.

"Honey, had me worried that the babies would be scarred or something," Mrs. Tate said kissing little Aiden on his cheek.

"Baby, I had Dr. Hawkins on speed dial for the therapy sessions they would require at a year old!" Charlene hooted.

"Oh, stop it. It was my hormones I love these *little terrors,*" she said for good measure then laughed.

"Oh Lord, poor babies. Can you find more appropriate nicknames for my nephews?" Caressa demanded.

"I'm just kidding seriously," Rachel promised.

"Okay, so now that the babies are here safely, when are we gonna ride up on the bitch that forced their early arrival?" Charlene cracked her knuckles and did a quick stretch.

"Listen, I'm ready and since these little ah…see got y'all, anyway since the babies aren't on the tit, I can ride any time. How long is everyone here?" Rachel looked around at her circle.

"For about a week" Jocelyn provided.

"Alright cool, I'm good to go anytime," Rachel said as Dashawn pinned her with a look. "What babe? That bitch got it coming and I told her ass that I would see her again. So you might as well get ready to get your daddy daycare on cause her ass-whooping is about to be delivered."

"Son, while I don't condone violence, I think Rachel is justified this time. That little girl caused her to go into pre-term labor, and while your sons are good now, they spent about a week in the NICU," his mother concluded as the voice of confirmation.

Rachel nodded. "Thank you, Mrs. Tate. I just read something on Instagram not too long ago that said, *No one ever notices when you're being provoked, just when you retaliate.* Well, in the words of Madea. "It's time to GET THAT FOOL. Who's ready to ride?"

"While I'm all for you handling your business Love, can it wait until our babies are a little older?" Dashawn asked her.

"While I'm all for you playing the peacemaker, it's time for my two piece to make itself present. The boys are two weeks old, safe, and healthy. Now I will beat her ass and be home in time for their next feeding. Come on girls," she said passing Jayden to Dashawn.

CHAPTER TWENTY-FOUR

Charlene drove the women including Rachel over to Rachel's father's house where her half-sister Nisha visited every day about this time. Rachel knew this as it had come up in some of her conversations with her dad. "Let's hang out here for a little bit because I don't want my dad to get in the middle of this or feel like he needs to take sides. We can catch up while we wait," she suggested.

"Girl, you want us to sit here in this vehicle in front of this house and expect that nobody will call the damn cops?" Reia asked looking around.

"Pretty much, I don't anticipate her staying in there too long as I'm going to call my dad and pretend that I'm bringing the babies over to see him. That will cause her to leave sooner as he won't want the conflict. Hold on," she said dialing his number. "Hey Dad, how are you? Good, good, yep we came home a few days ago. I want to bring them by to see you. Uh huh, now. I can be there in about thirty to forty-five minutes. Ok, see you then," she told him hanging up.

"What are you gonna do when that time comes and goes with you not showing up?" Jocelyn inquired.

"Oh, I'll just call and tell him something came up," she nonchalantly replied watching the front door.

"Smart. So, while we wait, how was your labor and stuff? You haven't really filled us in, although we heard how Dashawn teeter-tottered and hit the floor," Reia hollered with laughter.

"Worst pain ever and two at one time was a nightmare. Oh, and I ripped so bad I'm still scared to look at myself in the mirror. I'm just hoping that it's still presentable down there." She chuckled.

"It doesn't matter, Dashawn is probably counting down the time until he can get back in it. He won't care what it looks like as long as he still has an option to stroke it." Charlene snickered.

"What I tell you? Here she comes." Rachel pointed toward the door as Nisha walked down the steps toward her car parked on the street. "Time to enact my revenge, watch for my dad and don't let him stop this if he comes out," she told the girls as she hurriedly got out of the vehicle and ran up on her sister punching her in the mouth without exchanging one word.

"Well damn, I guess she didn't come to talk," Jocelyn said as they rushed out of the vehicle.

"She sure the fuck didn't, she is whooping ass and taking names," Charlene said as they stood watching Rachel deliver blow after blow.

Nisha tried fighting back, but her swings were miscalculated and ill-timed and Rachel blacked out as she remembered how helpless her babies looked in the NICU. "Bitch, I told you that I was coming for your ass, didn't I?" she exclaimed continuing to swing and connect.

"Oh my God, should we stop this yet?" Monica asked as they allowed Rachel to continue beating the shit out of her sister.

"I'd like to see you *try* to stop her," Caressa happily expressed. "I'm not sure she would recognize you if you interfered right now and you'd catch a few of those hands too. So, nope that bitch asked for this."

Dashawn bounced Jayden as he walked back and forth around the perimeter of the house trying to get him to calm down. It had been an hour and Rachel wasn't back yet, nor was she answering her phone. He was beginning to worry, and Jayden didn't want anybody. His comfort level was gone and it seemed as if he knew his mom was gone because they couldn't get him to eat, sleep, or be calm. Bouncing him helped for a little while, but he continually whimpered. "I know buddy, she'll be back soon," he told his son wondering what was happening. *Where is she? I hope she's okay and not in jail.*

Rachel, her group of friends and cousin entered the house a few minutes later, boisterously happy and cackling. "Monica, you know I told her what it was going to be when I got to her. I make no apology for any of it." She lifted her head in the air defiantly.

"So, I take it you handled your business, and all is right in the world?" Dashawn investigated as he bounced an antsy Jayden.

"Without a doubt, what did you do to my love muffin? Come to momma sweetie." She reached for the baby who quieted down as soon as he was in her arms.

"See, that's that bullshit right there!" Dashawn pouted.

"Stop being jealous of your son when he causes you to split in two then you can have his attention. Isn't that right love muffin? Momma knows," she cooed at the baby ignoring the looks she was receiving from everyone.

"Well, I'm glad that you're back, so we can discuss something else of importance," Mrs. Tate presented.

"Oh, what would that be, Mrs. Tate?" Rachel replied.

"Your wedding. Are you two still going to get married? The babies are here so when is the wedding to seal the deal?' she quizzed.

"How about we discuss it amongst ourselves first and then we'll inform you all after?" Dashawn recommended.

"I like that idea," Rachel agreed. "I hate to run you all out of here, but I'm tired and want to put the boys down for the night. Dashawn and I are grateful for you all and appreciate your being here but now it's time for us to bid you all ado," she communicated not so subtly.

"Alrighty then, what a way to say you've worn out your welcome… now get to stepping!" Charlene teased.

"I'm happy that you made it home without a trip to central booking first." Dashawn shook his head. "How did it go? You know little man doesn't do well without you being close to him. I don't know what you're going to do when it's time for you to return to work and he won't stay at daycare," he grumbled to her.

"I know. Can you see why I wasn't a fan of them being titty babies, imagine how attached both would be if that were the case. Hmmph. as far as how things went, how do you think? I kindly waited for that bitch to step out of my dad's house and I gave her what I should have weeks ago. She didn't know what hit her… *literally.*" Rachel finished snickering.

"You realize that you're a mother now and you can't go around serving up ass whooping's and things." He gave her a semi-serious look… unconvincingly.

"Uh huh, this coming from the man who had extreme feelings about the situation as we sat in the NICU after the boys arrived. I still remember your loving encouragement," she expressed putting finger quotations around encouragement.

"Our son stopped breathing I would have said anything at that moment," Dashawn spoke interrupting the memory while remembering that day as well.

"Tell me about it, you told me to *kill that bitch* for causing this pain to us and the boys," she said.

"I sure did." He shrugged unrepentantly.

"Water under the bridge now. I didn't kill her, but I sure beat her ass good. Next time, she'll rethink her position on confronting me."

"Good, every time I think about that day my fucking blood boils." He growled.

"It's over for now, how about we go put the boys to bed and then head to bed ourselves? I'm beat."

A few hours later, Dashawn sat next to Rachel in her bed with each of them feeding a twin. It seemed as if the boys were in total sync, as one couldn't wake up for feeding without the other being up. It meant that they both had to be up together, instead of one of them sleeping for a little while or them taking turns.

"I was wondering if you had any thoughts of how you wanted to get married?" Dashawn probed.

"Haven't thought about it one way or another, to be honest." She shrugged.

Dashawn looked at her cross-eyed. "What do you mean you haven't thought about it? You are planning to marry me, right?"

"I suppose."

"Ok, I'm not sure I'm following you, and that thought alone is pissing me off. You told me before that you wouldn't marry me while you were pregnant. Well damn it, you aren't pregnant anymore, so I need more than *I suppose,*" he grumbled getting more upset as the minutes ticked by.

Rachel looked over at Dashawn and decided to quit taunting him as he looked to be holding on by a thread. "Don't get your boxers in a bunch, we're getting married. When would you like to make an honest woman out of me? You sure you're up for the twenty-four seven, seven days a week job? You know I'm not easy on any given day…" She peered at him as she burped the baby.

"I knew who you were when I put my ring on your finger. I also know with absolute assurance that I want to spend the rest of my loving the *HELL* out of you. So, the better question is when YOU would like to be made honest?" He raised his eyebrows at her with a piercing look.

"Uh-um, well, in that case, let's start planning. I don't want a big to-do, just something small and intimate between the people we love and us. We also need to discuss what we're going to do about our living arrangements. I don't think it'll look good to be married but living apart," she stated.

"You sure? It could be the key to that whole *happy wife, happy life* slogan," he suggested. Seeing the serious look on her face caused him to get serious. "Okay, okay! Just kidding. I can rent out my house if you want to stay here or you and the boys can move in with me. As long as I have my family, I don't give a damn where we reside. I also know the perfect place for us to get married, so I'll take care of booking the location. You handle showing up, can you handle that?"

"Nah, nope, no cigar. This is a partnership and I want equal investment into this thing, so how about we do it together and we allow our guests to simply show up?" she posed.

"I tried, but I like the idea so how about I drive you past the location after work tomorrow and we see if it's available? Since you want something small but intimate, I think we can pull something together in no time. The question is how are we gonna pull a wedding together while caring for two newborns?" He scratched his head in thought.

"Baby, one thing is for sure, I might be an only child born to my mother, but I've been blessed with four fierce friends and one badass cousin who make up my team. You also have your parents and brother that can pitch in. Oh, and you have that pain in my ass," she finished.

"You know I was following you all the way up until the pain in the ass part Love. Why don't you like Ronnie? And you know that Jonathan has been distant, so he may not do it. Hell, I'm not sure when the last time we've even spoken was," he pondered.

"You know Ronnie works my damn nerves with his indecisive ass he's been stringing along poor Shauna since we've been together, and they were together before we even met. On top of that, he thinks he's a Mack daddy, don't his dumb ass know that women eat Mack daddies for brunch? I also think now is a good time for you to bridge the gap between you and your brother. He needs to be in not only your life but the boy's life as well. It doesn't make sense and as much as you've been on me about getting my life together, I've forgotten about the missing link in your chain. It's time Dashawn, family is everything..." she stopped getting emotional.

Damn, when did Rachel's mean ass get so emotional all of a sudden? Dashawn was looking at Rachel, but his mind was miles away, as he remembered that it had been close to a year and a half since he'd seen or heard from his brother. After their last conversation, he'd decided to give him some room, but Rachel was right, family was everything, and maybe it was time to quit allowing his brother to be separated from the family...

... "Hey man, thanks for stopping by. I wanted to see how you're doing mom told me you came by last week but left before I got there. What's up with you?" Dashawn asked looking at his brother.

"What I do bro? I've meant to call you but I-uh, been traveling a lot for work these days," Jonathan said without meeting his eyes.

"Traveling huh? So where have you been going or is that the excuse you're using to continue avoiding me?" he probed.

"Listen, I don't need this shit it's bad enough coming from Ma, so miss me with the bullshit a'ight?" Jonathan raised his voice.

"Then, get your fucking head out of your ass. He's gone and distancing yourself won't bring him back!" Dashawn yelled back.

"Fuck you, Shawn. This shit has always been hard for me, and there's no timetable on grief," he spat.

"I know but don't you think it hurts Mom for you to pull away like this? Dad's been gone for many years now, and Mom has been remarried and happy. What made you decide to start bunching your gotdamn draws in separation NOW?" he growled pissed by the situation.

Jonathan stood in a defensive stance heaving and fighting for control. "I don't answer to you, and I'll do what the FUCK I feel is necessary for my own survival. Now BACK.THE.FUCK.OFF." he snarled as he turned and headed for the door.

"Come on man, don't do this shit. We're better than this right here," Dashawn said trying to gain control of his temper.

"I got to go Shawn, and since my job has actually picked up, I'll be traveling a lot," Jonathan said as he stormed out of the house slamming the door as he went.

"MOTHERFUCKER!" Dashawn yelled frustrated by how things went with his younger brother.

CHAPTER TWENTY-FIVE

That blow up with his brother was over a year ago, and he hadn't seen or heard from him. Rachel had made a valid point. Enough time had passed it was time to resolve some issues and get his brother back. Their father had died suddenly of a massive heart attack and it seemed as if Jonathan never recovered. When his mother married James three years after his passing, Jonathan became even more distant, but he was still present up until roughly the same time as his cruise and his dating Rachel. *No time like the present.* Dialing his brother's number, he prayed for a better outcome than the last one they had. "Uh, hey bro. How are you man?" he hesitated when the call connected.

"Sup, Shawn. I'm uh-alright, how are you?" Jonathan slowly returned.

"Good man, listen. Enough time has passed between us, and I hate how we left things. A lot has happened in my world, and I'm sure in yours as well. For one, you're an uncle to two nephews, and I'm getting married," he informed him.

"Oh wow, damn man congrats on both accounts. Damn, I'm uh, damn man. I've been missing a lot in your life. This shit doesn't feel good right now, although it never did. I'm sorry for how I handled that day. Ma has been on me about calling you. I just figured we weren't in that place yet."

"Fuck the bullshit, Jonathan. We're brothers, and that shit wasn't important and not enough for us to be exempt from each other's life and definitely not for this long."

"Yeah, you're right. So, two kids and marriage? Wow, Shawn."

"Right, man they're twins and almost a month old. Keeping Rachel and me on our toes for sure." He chuckled.

"Twins? Double trouble huh? I bet you're a good father like ours was," he choked up a little.

"I try. Listen man, I know Dad left us suddenly but what's going with you? It's not easy for me, but I didn't know that I'd lose my brother in the process. I miss you dude." Dashawn grabbed his head as he held the phone tightly.

"I just had a hard time, and then when Mom married James, it made everything more final than the funeral did. I didn't know how to cope so pulling away was much easier, but in the meantime, I've missed so much of your life. Calling and talking to Ma every few weeks has been difficult," he finished.

"Yeah, I imagine it's been hard for her as well, although she hasn't talked to me about anything that you've discussed with her. She and I haven't brought up any of it actually which means that she's masking for the sake of appearances. But uh, forget all of that. I'm getting married and you must be in my wedding. You also need to meet your nephews and my Love," Dashawn said wiping the tears that had slipped out.

"For sure man, what's the boy's names? I'm so happy to hear that you're moving towards your happily ever after."

"Definitely, they're names are Aiden and Jayden. Rachel is my everything, man. I wouldn't be able to continue in this cruel world without her. Why don't you set some time aside and we'll hook up?"

"For sure. In the meantime, I've got to run heading back out of town. Thanks for reaching out to me Shawn. I love you bro," Jonathan expressed.

"That's what family is for. Love you back dude. Talk with you soon," Dashawn said hanging up.

Rachel had gotten up when Dashawn began talking to his brother, so they could have some privacy. She hoped they could reconcile and get past their differences, she meant what she said....family was everything, and it was essential to hold on to the ones you had. Staring out of the nursery window as she held Aiden, she smiled. She had her family.

Dashawn walked into the nursery hugging her with one arm while being careful of their son. "So, how did it go?" she asked.

"I finally understand where his head is, and he agreed to meet the boys and you. I also told him that I want him at the wedding. So, I think we can do this now. Let's get married within the next six months, is that long enough for us to plan?" he asked.

"If we go the small, intimate route, I'm sure we could totally pull it off. Let's do it babe," she happily replied.

"Cool, six months from now you'll finally be Mrs. Dashawn Sanders. Now go ahead and put little man in his bed and let's go celebrate!" he boasted then squeezed her tight, kissed her forehead and headed out of the nursery.

"Now Rachel, I need you to keep an open mind," Dashawn was saying as they pulled into the gravel drive of Sloan Barn and Estates.

"Depends on what I see once we get out of this car, cause I'm not sure about this," she returned as they drove down the long driveway.

"I promise you it will be everything you want and need it to be, trust me." He lightly squeezed her hand.

"Uh huh, we'll see about—" she stopped as the trees parted, and they drove closer to a beautiful red barn.

"You were saying," he asked as he pulled into the parking lot and cut the engine.

Rachel couldn't say anything as he grabbed the double stroller and proceeded to put their sons in, then came and opened her door so she could get out. "Wow, this is a very nice barn."

"Wait until you see the inside and the area out back, you'll love it even more."

Walking up the front steps, Rachel smiled as she noted the beautiful flowers that surrounded the area in the front of the building. Entering the barn, she indicated that there was an open area with restrooms off to the immediate right, there was a sitting area and fireplace. Just past the sitting area was a fully furnished kitchen area that made her smile as she'd wondered how she could handle food for her reception. As they continued walking past the kitchen, they turned the corner where you could either go up the steps or take an elevator to the next level. Seeing as they had the twins, they took the elevator, and a small gasp escaped her mouth as she took in the converted barn. It was a vast open floor plan with another fireplace that served as the focal point. It was the perfect place to hold their intimate reception. "Wow, I love this place," she told Dashawn.

"I figured you might, and this room can be set up any way we want, I thought that the area just in front of the fireplace could be reserved as the dance floor. The head table could be set up over there by the windows, and then we could have round tables set up around the room. How does that sound to you?"

"Sounds like I need to let you take the lead, I think you have it handled. Now show me the wedding ceremony location. I'm excited."

"No problem you're going to love this part," he said as they stepped back on the elevator and proceeded back down to exit the building.

A few minutes later, Rachel was smiling harder as she imagined the day that she would become Mrs. Dashawn Sanders. "This is perfect, please tell me you booked it?" she said as she looked at the area behind the barn that had a pond with a bridge overpass. The area seemed to be set up for a wedding as there was an arch in front of the lake creating a backdrop as chairs lined both sides of a staged aisle.

Two weeks before his wedding day, Dashawn sat on the couch watching the boys play in the playpen, contemplating how much his life was about to change. He'd introduced his brother to Rachel and the boys a few days after their phone conversation. They'd decided to stay in Rachel's house, since her and the boys were the most comfortable here. Looking at his ringing phone, he picked it up. "Yeah, what's up?"

"So, I've been told that you're not having a bachelor party and I'm trying to figure out why," Caressa's husband Brian drilled. "Shit man, you know our women are going to have a bachelorette party, so how come you're not following suit?"

"Well, somebody has to stay with the boys since they're so young and I decided that it would be me. So, we're going to have a daddy party while our women go turn up. You don't like that idea though?" he asked laughing.

"Man, I swear I think Rachel took your balls and placed them in the meat grinder. How the fuck you got the women having a bachelorette party and propose a gotdamn daddy party for us? You done lost your mind dude!" Brian ranted.

"Sorry dude, but your son is older so leaving him with somebody isn't that big a deal. My little men are only seven months we're not quite ready to leave them with anybody." He laughed at his friends' expense.

"Man, this shit is far from funny, and your mom is present in your life so what the hell kind of cornball shit is this you're beating my ears with?" Brian continued.

"Calm down man, I feel like I'm talking to a woman right now. Did you just get off your rag or something?" he teased.

"Oh, so now that's what we not gonna do right now? My job has been stressing me out lately, and I just knew you'd have a bachelor party for us to unwind and get our male bonding on. Now we on pussy ass babysitting duty? This is some bullshit. Let me hit up the other fellas and bring them up to speed. I'll see yo ass next week with my son," he finished.

"A'ight, I'll see you next week dude." Dashawn chuckled disconnecting the call while shaking his head at his friend's antics.

Meanwhile, Rachel was sitting over at Charlene's house reminiscing about a variety of things when she remembered an encounter she had in college. "Oh God, did I ever tell you about the experience I had when I was in college with that guy I was dating?" she asked snickering from memory.

"No, but I remember the douchebag, what was his name, John, Paul, Sebastian, shit, what was his name?" Charlene snapped her fingers trying to jog her memory.

Unable to hold it in any longer, Rachel began laughing. "Damon, girl I nicknamed him, *The Fumbler* because he perfected the concept. I thought for sure he was going to bring it. Instead, I felt like Carrie Bradshaw from *Sex in the City,* in that episode where she had jackrabbit sex. He banged me against his headboard to the point of real stars in my eyes. Girl, it was awful. Oh, and that's *AFTER* he nearly stabbed my cooch to death trying to find the right hole. What a damn tragedy because he had a nice package. He just had no clue what to do with it I should have been like the plane taxi directors and directed myself into a proper orgasm. Instead of spending two nights in bed icing my damn neck."

Charlene was laughing so hard tears were streaming down her face. "You're a damn fool, did you just compare it to Carrie Bradshaw's experience?" she finished wiping her eyes.

"Tell me about it, and then I had to dodge his ass on campus after that while he bragged about us having mind-blowing sex. After the sixth woman asking me about how he was and the male harassment I was getting, I snapped." She looked away.

"Oh shit, what did you do or better yet what did you say?" Charlene scooted to the edge of her couch.

"I said his dick was so small I didn't recall him ever getting it in because a pinky kept stabbing my pussy. I couldn't help myself after his boys kept hounding me and other guys were trying to be my next conquest..." she stopped barely holding onto her laughter.

"Good for you and it served his no stroke having ass right!" Charlene laughed slapping fives with her. "After all of that, here you are, a week away from marrying your baby's daddy. I'm so happy for you cousin." She smiled wide.

"I know, I can't believe it myself, and he's uh-never mind too much info. I love him so much and am honored that he chose me…" She stared off dreamily.

"Please, you're worth choosing, despite the rough hand you were dealt. Love you Rachel and don't ever doubt your worth," Charlene said as she enveloped Rachel in a tight embrace.

"Aww, thank you, cousin. I love you too. You have been my rock. I'm sorry if I've been anything but the same to and for you," she stated as her voice cracked.

"If you don't get your ass outta here, you damn sure shouldn't be apologizing about shit!" Charlene looked at her as if she was crazy.

"Just want you to know how much I love and appreciate you for all that you are in my life. Now, let me rescue the boys from their dad. See you later cousin," she said kissing and hugging her.

"What do you mean Brian called you mad about the Daddy Bachelor Party? Brian is usually laid back and reserved?" Rachel asked him laughing from his story recant.

"He wasn't *reserved* today. I just wish I could have seen his actual facial expression because he was undoubtedly pissed with me. It made my rough work day a little lighter, to be honest. You know none of that matters to me though, and you know how I feel about people with the boys right now," Dashawn unapologetically stated.

"I know how overprotective you are, and you know that only your mother would keep them. She would love the opportunity to smother them more than she already does. Are you sure you don't want to have a traditional party, it is your last hurrah after all?" She stared at him skeptically.

"Yeah, I'm sure, my last hurrah happened on that cruise after I had you in my bed. I have everything that I need right here," he replied.

"I didn't say go out and have one last fling or romp before getting married, but don't men go to strip clubs and stuff before they attach the chain to the ball?"

"Not all of us, besides it'll be fun to bond with our children that could still be a fun night."

"Uh huh, tell me anything, but none of that sounds like fun. I think you've been watching way too many kiddie movies these days. You're going to lose your player and man card over this shit." She laughed at him.

Dashawn just looked at her as he tried to keep a straight face *and* his plans under wraps. He also thanked the man above for the woman that he set out to make a fling that turned into his everything. Despite the things that she'd been through, she still persevered and got back up after many knockouts. He loved her motivation to push and watching her with his sons made him love her even more. “How about I remind you why that type of party isn’t important to me?” he huskily suggested.

“What do you have in mind?” she inquired as she watched him stalk toward her.

“I can show you better than I can tell you, Love,” he said as he took her lips in a fierce kiss.

Rachel moaned into his mouth as she lost any form of response. Caring for the twins didn’t provide many times for intimacy, so any opportunity they could get to connect, she stayed ready. “Mmm,” she moaned as he began kissing down her neck causing goosebumps to form on her skin.

“You’re wearing too many clothes,” he said removing the nightshirt she’d changed into after her shower. When he realized that she was bare underneath, he growled. “Nothing more beautiful than the body of the woman who’s carried two of my children.”

Rachel stood in front of him noting how his brown eyes sparkled with desire and love causing her to leak. “Dashawn…” she groaned.

Dashawn quickly removed his pajama pants and swooped down picking her up forcing her to wrap her legs around his waist. Backing up, he leaned her up against the dresser and slid into his home base cautious of his speed as well as the pressure. “Feels like heaven, Love,” he breathed as he slowly penetrated her.

Rachel held onto him enjoying the speed that he was moving and the love that she saw in his eyes. She didn’t know that she could ever experience complete and unconditional love, but Dashawn was a welcome addition to her life. As he reminded her of his love and adoration, she basked in the feel of him deep inside of her. With every push, she grew more excited causing additional lubrication. "OH, baby…" she whimpered.

"I've got you…" Dashawn moaned as he continued making love to her. He breathed deep and released inside of her, whispering her name, "Rachel."

After a joint shower, Rachel laid in bed comforted by the rise and fall of Dashawn's chest. She couldn't believe that as an abused and neglected child, she would wind up with so many blessings. Laying here with her man made her overjoyed with gratitude. "Love you Dashawn," she whispered.

"Love you more, Love. Now go to sleep," he grumbled gripping her tighter around her waist.

CHAPTER TWENTY-SIX

Thursday night before the wedding festivities, Dashawn prepared to say bye to Rachel. They would be separated until their wedding day. "The next time I see you will be when I watch you strut towards our happy ending. Have fun at your last hurrah, Love." He kissed her neck and then her lips.

"I look forward to meeting you on our personal white carpet, babe. Enjoy your *Daddy* party," she sarcastically teased.

"Oh, I will. I have a nice party planned for the sourpuss men who have the honor of joining me." He gave her a sneaky grin.

"Sounds good, see you later," she returned ignoring his grin as she left the house.

Dashawn smirked as he walked back into the house closing the door. He headed towards the kitchen to prepare the food for the guys, but shortly after… the doorbell rang. *Damn, somebody is early and anxious to party.* Arriving at the door, he opened it and greeted his first guest. "What's up, Lamont? Glad you made it. Come on in." He opened the door wide allowing him to enter.

"Of all people to get married, I didn't expect it to be you, Shawn. I'm tripping that somebody actually agreed to put up with you for a lifelong sentence," Lamont said walking in the house carrying his overnight bag. "Where am I setting up, so I can put this bag down?"

"We're all going to be camping out back. I have tents and things set up already. It'll be the boy's first campout with Dad," he proudly expressed.

Lamont just stood there staring at him for a minute. "Did your sappy ass just say we're having a campout and with your babies?"

"I sure did, and it should be lit."

Lamont stared at him some more, like he was an alien with two heads. "The only thing lit about this shit will be the fire and don't think we're going to sit around singing Kumbaya or no pansy shit like that. By the way, what time are the women coming through tomorrow night?"

"Did you miss the statement about my sons being here? There won't be any strippers coming through," Dashawn deadpanned with a straight face as he washed the chicken he was about to cook.

"Nothing says father and son bonding like stripper madness, my dude!" Lamont joked.

"You stupid, man. Aiden and Jayden are only seven months, and short of trying to search out their next milk fix, they wouldn't know the first thing about no strippers!" Dashawn laughed boisterously.

Rachel and her bridesmaids spent all day Thursday getting prepared for the wedding. She even had her final dress fitting which made her smile with tears streaming down her face. "It's so beautiful," she said as she watched her seamstress complete the last-minute adjustments. *I wish I had a Mom here and happy for me right now.*

"You know at any time, I can whisk you out of here, and you don't have to do this right?" Charlene posed.

"Girl, if you don't stop. Hell, I'm waiting for you to settle down and start popping out babies of your own" she told her cousin wiping her eyes.

"Now, you tripping for real. Just because you and these other ladies ran towards that rainbow of wedded bullshit—I mean bliss, doesn't mean that everybody should. I'm perfectly fine having the ability to get random ass any time I feel like it," Charlene proudly stated.

"I can't wait to see somebody change all of those words while making you eat them!" Caressa chimed in.

"Hell, I'm still stuck at her having babies!" Reia laughed.

"What happened to Mark? Y'all on the outs again?" Rachel asked analyzing Charlene's words.

"Honey, I never told you this, but Mark is my honorary booty stand in. Any time I feel the need to sweat out my sheets, I dial a dick and *poof* one shows up in the form of Mark," she teased.

"Is he coming to the wedding to see you or burn up your sheets later that night?" Monica asked.

"Nope, wanted to keep my options open in case Dashawn has any single friends for me to trade his ass in for."

"You're a mess girl, but I love you." Jocelyn smirked adding to the conversation.

"Yeah, whatever. I love y'all too. Now, let's get off here before you get too much happy and wedding mess on me. I'm starting to itch as it is," Charlene finished while rubbing her arms.

"Only my damn cousin would make fun of brides and weddings the day before the last day of her cousin's wedding. I can't deal with you fool!" Rachel hollered with laughter.

Friday afternoon Dashawn dropped the twins off to his mother and continued to plan one of his last hurrahs. As he drove the rented van full of his groomsmen, he heard grumblings coming from the back causing him to chuckle internally. *These dudes.*

"We might have to revoke his *man card* after this! I can't believe he had us roasting motherfucking marshmallows and shit last night. No strippers either, what kind of fucking bachelor party is this anyway?" Ronnie ranted.

"It's like Rachel snipped his punk ass before she left yesterday. I'm almost ashamed to be seen with his pansy ass." Lamont shook his head disgusted.

"Aw, stop messing with him fellas, when you two settle down, you'll understand." Carter smirked.

"Nah, the only thing settling down with me will be my stomach after I eat!" Ronnie kidded as he gave Lamont dap.

Pulling up to a remote location with a steel framed building in front, Dashawn parked the van and looked in the rearview mirror. "Nice to know y'all got my back, let's go. We'll see who's the pansy momentarily."

"What kind of desert mission you got us going on?" Justin asked looking around uncomfortably.

"Seeing as how I'm going to be taking the ultimate plunge tomorrow, I thought I would get a head start today." Dashawn smirked as they entered the building.

"Oh shit, you're about to skydive? That's insane! Rachel will kill us if you don't show up or if you even get a hangnail. But whatever, sign me up this looks like fun," Myles said entering the conversation.

"Hell, yeah!" a few more of the men cheered.

"See, this kind of makes up for the lack of strippers tonight, doesn't it?" Dashawn grinned sneakily.

"Keep telling yourself that man!" Lamont laughed as the guys began teasing him.

Driving back to the house after their skydiving adventure...

"Man, that was epic. I had no idea I would enjoy it so much!" Ronnie yelled excitedly still on a high from the experience.

"Uh huh," Dashawn nonchalantly replied as he pulled into the driveway back at the house, smirking as he saw his stepfather James' car along with an unknown car on the street. "Come on pansies, time for more

Kumbaya!" he laughed. Entering the house, he heard Jodeci's Freak'n You playing.

"FUCK!" Lamont yelled as he saw the two strippers slowly gyrating to the music as they entered the living room.

"Guess he earned his right to keep his *man card,*" Justin said as the women approached them.

"Hey boys, why don't you come on in and we'll help you take a load off. I'm Dimples and this is Sunshine."

Dimples looked slim and thick with perky breasts that were straining in the silk negligee she wore. Sunshine was thicker with large breasts, and she wore a yellow cat suit with a black belt tied around her waist. She slowly tapped her right hand with a bright yellow whip.

"If I get to play with you two, I'm the motherfucking bachelor tonight," Ronnie stated peering at the women so hard he looked like he would faint.

"Who's the damn pansy now? Get your ass together, dude. Show these women some respect." Dashawn growled pushing him along.

"Alright, my job here is done. Let me go help your mom with the babies Dashawn. Have a good time fellas and remember we need to be up early," James said giving Dashawn dap as he walked towards the door.

"Alright handsome, we've been made aware that you're the man of the hour, so our job tonight is to make you regret spending the night separated from your fiancé," Sunshine told him as she cracked her whip.

"It's about to go down now," Brian cheered as he grabbed a seat to take in the show.

In a hotel in an undisclosed location...

"This damn room is nice, who was in charge of set up?" Caressa asked looking around the suite.

"Charlene and Jocelyn took care of setting up," Rachel said sipping on her wine.

"Should have known Charlene had some input with all of the tiny dicks scattered everywhere. Who knew you could get dick shaped lipstick, this is unreal!" Reia teased.

"Uh, actually those were supplied by me, and you should have seen the looks I got from the airline personnel after scanning my carryon bag!" Jocelyn laughed.

"Hey, a little dick goes a long way. Try this dick pop it's pretty good," Charlene joked as she held the cake pop shaped penis in Rachel's face.

"First of all, it looks like you have cum oozing down your mouth, wipe your damn face. Secondly, nope pass on the little dick," Rachel said as she slapped fives with her assistant, Megan.

"OK!" the other women echoed.

A few hours later, the women were having a blast and were playing *Pin the Macho on the Man* while stumbling from their slightly tipsy state. Their pins and objects were pinned in places that gave pause as well as caused loud laughter with each turn taken. Before the final pin was made, a knock sounded at the door.

"I'll get it." Monica smirked walking towards the door.

"MERCY!" Megan screamed grabbing her chest as two muscular men walked into the room. The first guy was a dark skinned man with dreads wearing leather chaps, a black muscle shirt showcasing his impressive biceps and steel toe boots. The second guy was the color of a perfectly brewed latte. He was bald with a full beard wearing gray sweatpants, a wife beater, and tennis shoes.

"Good evening ladies," they said with thick Southern accents.

"It is now," Charlene replied licking her lips.

"We're looking for Monica," Mr. Latte said looking around the room with a devilish smile.

"That would be me handsome." Monica waved her hand stepping from behind them.

After a brief chat, they began setting up to start their set. "It's our understanding that one of you are getting married tomorrow," leather dressed dude said.

"Guilty as charged," Rachel spoke up hesitantly.

Licking his lips he replied, "Damn, he's a lucky sonofabitch. Come sit here Sweetheart, let's see if we can make you change your mind," Mr. Latte said reaching for her hand as the other guy stood behind a chair in the center of the room.

"Before we continue, let's make some introductions. My name is Midnight," the guy in leather said. "And this is Sensation, he pointed to gray sweats. It'll be our pleasure to give you ladies multiple Sensations up till Midnight."

"Baby, you about to make me change my mind and I'm not even the bride-to-be!" Charlene teased.

Fanning her face, a little, Rachel sat down in the chair praying that she could make it through this experience with her dignity intact. As they began to dance and remove clothes, she wondered if she could get through the night without jumping on them. *Gotdamn!*

"HAVE MERCY?" Jocelyn said echoing the thoughts around the room as Sensation stripped down to nothing but a thin cloth hanging from his crotch.

"Lawd, you can say that again," Rachel said as he began slowly coming her way. *I'm getting married. I'm getting married.* "Y'all, please keep me from embarrassing myself," she said as Sensation straddled her as his dick moved unclothed between her legs.

"Oh damn, I'm getting married too!" Charlene screamed.

"I love my man," Rachel chanted when Sensation got up giving her and her lap a quick reprieve. But the reprieve was temporary as Midnight grabbed her hand, while Sensation removed the chair. Midnight then picked her up and dropped down on the floor as he eased her up and down on his cock that was uncovered, long, and hard. Then Sensation got behind her straddling her ass slowly pumping into her. "Oh, my gawd!" she moaned.

"It's a good thing she's wearing clothes, shit!" Kayla exclaimed.

"Well, I'll be damned!" Megan screeched.

"Right, I'm pretty sure she has second thoughts now," Caressa teased.

"Nope, I'm sure she is too damn wet to be thinking anything," Reia provided.

"Damn. They asses need to do that with me next!" Charlene pouted.

Minutes later, a disheveled looking Rachel sipped her wine. "It's going to be a long night."

CHAPTER TWENTY-SEVEN

Dashawn, his groomsmen, stepfather James, his mom and his sons arrived at the wedding location two hours before the ceremony was set to begin. Dashawn wanted to inspect the grounds to make sure that everything was in place. The wedding and reception were going to be held at the same place. A few months before proposing to Rachel, somebody had brought the location to his attention. After seeing it and talking to Rachel – confirming her desire for something small and intimate – he knew it would be the perfect location. He remembered the way she had looked when she first saw it. They were in total agreement. It was THE place.

"Oh, my gosh! This place is so cute," his mother said as they entered the room designated as his holding spot.

"Yeah, I think it's perfect," he said kissing his son's cheeks as they slumbered in the double stroller, they were put in after they got out of the limo.

"Are you really bout to get married here? Where is my boy, because this isn't his speed?" Lamont griped.

Laughing, Dashawn looked at his friend as he shook his head at his antics. "This place is perfect and shows how much you know. I suggested this spot to Rachel, and after she saw it, she approved."

"Bro, how on earth could your wife-to-be approve this place? It's a barn for goodness sake!" Jonathan said looking at his brother strangely.

Dashawn knew for sure that his woman approved so he wasn't bothered by this. "Come on Jonathan, you're acting like this knucklehead. Besides, the wedding is outside and the reception will take place in the barn but wait until you see it set up. You'll be changing your mind and apologizing." He gave him a Cheshire grin.

"Not sure I would go that far, but we'll see in a little while. Are you nervous, man?" Jonathan asked.

Looking at his groomsmen as they all surrounded him, he replied, "Not in the least. If I don't know anything else, I know that woman was made for me and her agreeing to be my wife was one of the greatest moments of my life," he boasted.

"When did your son get so sappy, Mrs. Tate? This cat is not quite the one you raised nor the one that caused so much ruckus in college with me," Ronnie said looking at Dashawn's mom.

"I'm not falling into that trap, let me get out of here and go check on Rachel. You got my babies, Son?" She raised her eyebrows questioningly.

"You do know they're my sons, right Ma? Of course, I got them, and can you give Rachel this note for me please?" he asked handing her a piece of paper.

Rachel and her bridesmaids pulled up to the beautiful grounds of Sloan Barn and Estates, and her smile grew as she thought about the vows she'd be exchanging with Dashawn. She couldn't wait to see how the barn was transitioned into their reception area. She remembered thinking how crazy it was for a barn to be a wedding location. Her mind took her back to their tour of the grounds and barn making her smile. It surprised her and made her happy when Dashawn had given her that tour.

"You ready for this? I can still get you out of here," Charlene kidded snapping into Rachel's distant thoughts.

"I'm pretty sure it's too late for that now," Mrs. Tate said laughing as she entered the room.

"Hi, Mrs. Tate. How are my boys?" Rachel hugged her soon to be mother in law.

"The boys are good, they were sleeping when I left them, but they sure look cute in their little tuxedos. Oh, before I forget Shawn wanted me to give you this," she said handing her the note Dashawn had given her.

Rachel opened the note as she walked to the couch to sit down. With each word, her heart expanded and so did her eyes as the tears fell.

Today is the day that you will finally become my wife, and it fills me with so much emotion, passion, and excitement. I never knew that what started off as a chance attempt at one night would turn into one lifetime. Today, in front of God and everyone that's a part of our lives, I'm going to make my vows to you without restraint. I can't wait for you to become my happily ever after. Today begins the best days of our lives. See you at the altar.

Dashawn

"It's a damn good thing she isn't wearing makeup yet, damn he got her crying already," Her assistant, Megan kidded.

"Shut up girl, help me get dressed. I'm ready to meet my man at that altar," she said wiping her eyes as she headed to the partition.

"Yes, I've been dying to see you in your dress girl. That's one of the bad things about living out of state," Jocelyn said as everyone busied themselves with getting ready.

A short while later, Rachel was in her gown and ready to step out. "Ok, I'm ready and coming out." She stepped from behind the petition as the ladies all grinned wide.

"You look so beautiful Rachel, and that dress looks fabulous on you," Caressa told her.

Rachel had kept the dress a secret from everybody, as she wanted to have something that everybody witnessed on the day of and not way before the day. She'd chosen a bliss tulle A-line gown with an illusion lace halter neckline over a sweetheart hand-beaded lace applique bodice with a semi-sheer deep plunge. A lace racerback with a visible back bodice that had beaded hem lace on the front gathered skirt and vertical lace lines down the back skirt. It also had a chapel train. From the moment she'd seen the dress, she'd fallen in love with it, and it complimented her thick frame. Her hair was swept up into an elegant updo and she'd chosen natural looking makeup for a subtle look. “Thank you, ladies,” she said just as her dad entered the room.

“Wow! You look absolutely stunning Chelly. Thank you for the opportunity to give you away,” Lee said a little choked up.

“Thank you. I know that after that mess with Nisha and me you were caught in the middle but thank you for staying neutral. It couldn’t have been easy, and I’m glad to see you here on such a special day for me,” she returned trying not to cry.

“Now seriously, you do have makeup on now. Please don’t ruin it by crying!” Charlene begged.

“Come on, I think it’s showtime,” Rachel said ushering the women to the door to head to the ceremony.

Dashawn felt like the time would never come for the wedding to start but as the bridesmaids and groomsmen began walking down the aisle, he began to grow anxious. Then came the little ring bearers in the form of his sons, Aiden and Jayden who were being carried by their grandmother, who refused to allow anyone else the job. Next, came Maisha, the flower girl who was Kayla and Myles’ daughter and Rachel’s Goddaughter. Hearing the officiant give the “all rise” signal made his anxiety pique knowing Rachel was coming shortly. In the next couple of minutes, he heard ‘You Complete Me’ start to play, and he knew that Rachel’s feelings matched his own, as she’d secretly picked her entrance song.

Can you hear me out there…have you ever had someone who loved you…never leave your side…I know you'll be here…because you love me, yes, you do…

As she walked with her father towards him, he felt as if his heart was going to beat out of his chest. She was breathtaking. She was beautiful. She was his. Dashawn's face split into a broad smile as happiness he'd never felt before spread all throughout his body.

Walking towards Dashawn caused Rachel's eyes to water, as she noted the intense look on his face. His eyes met hers, and he held her captive as she mouthed the words to the song to him. She wanted him to know just how much the lyrics held true for her with him in her life. He completed her in every way, and if she never told him before now, she wanted him to know with assurance. As she stared into his eyes and mouthed the words, everyone else faded away.

I'm giving all my life and all my love, if you…promise me you'll be here forever…I'll give you me I'll give you everything…if you promise me you'll never leave me…

Rachel saw that his head was nodding up and down as he sung the lyrics, and it caused her heart to fill with love for this man. He had been her rock when many storms tried to destroy her, and she knew that no matter what happened… he would be with her. Once she reached him and her dad had expressed his being the person to give her away, she smiled at him. “Hi, babe,” she whispered.

“Hi Love,” Dashawn whispered back gripping her hand tightly.

As the officiant went through the motions of the ceremony, she couldn’t stop staring into the intensity of his eyes. In them, she saw love, peace, commitment, and happiness which was reinforced with the vows he gave her.

“Love, from the first sight of your pain and sorrow, I pledged that I had you. Well today, in front of God, our family and friends, I vow to you that I not only have you, but you can rest in knowing that everything you need is secure in me. I vow to be your protector, your rock, your comforter, your promise for better. I vow to complete you and NEVER leave your side,” he finished as he kissed her lips while wiping the tears tracking slowly down her face.

After prompting from the officiant and trying to gather her overflowing emotions, Rachel expressed her vows, “Today, in front of all these people, I vow to be your helpmate, I vow to be beside you through ups and downs. I vow to uplift and encourage you. I vow to submit to you even when I want to punch you in the face…” she paused at the sudden outburst of laughter. “I vow to build you up and never tear you down. I vow to honor and cherish you. I vow all of these things to you because you completed me when I least expected it. I make these vows to you knowing that you will love and cherish me as much as I do you for the rest of my life…” she stopped as she tried to prevent the overflow of tears.

After giving of rings and the last words of blessing from the officiant, she and Dashawn turned facing the audience as the officiant made their introduction.

"Ladies and gentlemen, I present to you, Mr. and Mrs. Dashawn Sanders. Dashawn, you may now kiss your bride."

Dashawn was a happy man as he looked at his wife, talking to her friends in the center of the barn. He couldn't help staring at her, she was stunning in her wedding dress, and he couldn't wait to get her out of it.

"Man, we know she's your wife now, but you realize that people are present right? Stop looking at her like you already have her naked in your bed," Ronnie grumbled.

"Jealousy is a dish best served cold motherfucker," Dashawn taunted back.

"Uh, I think the slogan is revenge is a dish best served cold. Quit making up shit!" Ronnie replied.

"Whatever. Stop sulking and if you stop acting like an ass, your turn will eventually come."

"Speaking of ass, who is the chick you paired me to walk down the aisle with?" Ronnie inquired.

"*Not interested in you*, is her name," Dashawn teased.

"Yeah, look at her she's looking at Lamont and probably don't know you're even in this room right now." Justin laughed.

"She's a pretty one, but that mouth might be more than I want to tame right now," Lamont stated looking at Charlene.

Laughing, Dashawn shook his head as he watched the women look at him and his group. "Looks like they're doing a lot of giggling and teasing at your expense, so I'm not sure if she's feeling you all that much either."

"It also sounds like Lamont is scared of her, so it's probably a good thing if she's not that interested," Brian spoke up.

"Trust me, y'all aren't ready for that one, probably best to walk away now," Dashawn said as he walked over towards Rachel, tired of the separation.

"Girl, look at his ass looking over here like he got something to offer. I eat men like him for breakfast he can't handle me," Charlene huffed as the women giggled.

"To me, looks like they're having a discussion about which of the two men you're going to end up with," Reia said.

"Hmmph, neither. I should have brought Mark for this shit. The one I walked down the aisle with kept leaning close to me as if he wanted to become my second skin or something," she ranted.

"Yeah, Ronnie is a bit much to take, and he thinks he's God's gift to women. I'd love to see you break his ass down to his tube socks," Rachel ranted.

"That would be hilarious to witness, oh but looks like it's not going to happen right now. It looks like Dashawn is stalking this way to reclaim his bride." Jocelyn nodded towards a purposed and driven Dashawn.

"Seems determined too, guess our girl time is temporarily suspended," Monica stated just as Dashawn reached them.

"Hey ladies, hope you're enjoying yourself. I'm stealing Mrs. Sanders from you now. I believe it's time for our first dance." He grabbed Rachel's hand leading her to the dance floor as the music began to play.

Forever…the love I have for you will last…forever…loving you always…forever.

Rachel leaned into the confines of Dashawn's chest feeling the manifestation of his love as *Forever* continued to play for their first dance.

I'm gonna give you everything you need…as long as I breathe…forever…

As the song ended, Rachel and Dashawn kept swaying caught up in their love for each other and ignoring everyone else in the room. She gazed into his eyes lovingly as he moved in to kiss her passionately causing thunderous clapping in the background. "Mmm," she moaned coming out of their bubble.

"Alright everyone, it's time for the father-daughter dance if Dashawn will let go of Rachel for a little bit," the announcer said.

Rachel watched her father come towards her, and she began to get emotional, their relationship hadn't transitioned as much as she liked, but she was hopeful that would change. As Luther Vandross' *Dance with My Father* streamed out the opening lines, her tears fell.

"Don't cry Chelly," Lee told her wiping her eyes with his thumb before he brought her to his chest and began moving.

"I don't mean to Dad, just a little uh, never mind. Thank you for being here," she whimpered.

"I know that I haven't been around or there for you and for that I'm sorry. The truth is I wasn't sure if I deserved to be in your life, so I've been scared to be involved. I'm happy that you allowed me an opportunity to see today and be a part of it. It's made my day, more than you know," Lee said as he paused to look at her.

"To be honest, part of me has been hesitant to build a real relationship with you out of fear of my mother. She put so much doubt in my mind about you that letting you off the hook before was easy. It hasn't been fair, and I'm glad that you stayed neutral with that Nisha situation cause anything else, would have made today a distant dream for the both of us."

"I tried to tell her to leave you alone because I knew you had some of yo momma in you. You whipped her good too." He smirked fighting his grin and laugh.

"She asked for it and I delivered that ass whooping fresh off babies delivered press." She full out laughed.

"I imagine she now knows that you two won't be mixing it up at any family reunions, no time soon. I understand and will remain neutral. I want to make another go of this relationship with you Chelly. Can we both try this time?" he pleaded.

"I will if you will," she replied, as the song ended not realizing it had been repeated when the DJ noticed their conversation. She hugged him and then walked off the dance floor with his arm around her shoulders.

CHAPTER TWENTY-EIGHT

"Where are we?" Rachel asked drowsily when Dashawn lightly shook her awake.

"Mrs. Q's Bed and Breakfast, where we'll be for the next two days. Let me help you, Love." He reached down into the car and swooped her up in his arms carrying her to their room.

"Uh, bed and breakfast? I thought we were headed home?" she fired back.

"Uh, we did just get married. The normal course of action is a honeymoon, and even though it'll be a short one, this is ours," he informed her after putting her down.

"Oh. Ok, babe. I don't have any clothes or anything to stay here for two days."

"Seeing as how we won't be leaving this room or the bed much, you won't need any. But I got you covered for the trip home," he huskily told her as he kissed her breathless while also slowly unzipping her gown. "I've been thinking about taking this off of you since I watched you strut towards me this afternoon."

Rachel grew fidgety as Dashawn began undressing her feeling the beginning tingles of her body's reaction to his touch. He was no longer her boyfriend and babies' daddy, he was her husband, and the thought alone made her cream which delighted him as he groped her pussy through her thong. "Ah…" she moaned.

"Looks like you've been anticipating me as much as I have you," he said as he slid the fabric to the side and inserted a finger into her. He started off slow and then began increasing his movements as she grew wetter. He added another digit causing her to cry out and grip his shoulders.

"Ooh, that feels good," she told him as she grabbed him through his pants and began pulling on him. "Stop for a second, take off your clothes," she panted removing her hand and pulling on his shirt in a hurry.

Once they were completely naked, Dashawn picked her up cradling her ass and threw her onto the center of the bed. He then dove in between her legs pushing them apart. Kissing her thighs, he made a slow path to her clit where he tongue kissed her. His tongue flattened as he inserted it in and out of her, alternating between kissing, sucking and biting. Tasting her repeatedly as he allowed his tongue to mimic his dick, driving her to the brink and then stopping before she reached her peak. "Nah, you won't be coming this way, Love. We got all night."

Rachel was trying to catch her breath when she was flipped on her stomach as Dashawn kissed her down her back. He began probing her rosette with two fingers using her wetness as a lubricant. She squirmed from the nervousness of being taken there. "Oh shit, Da-Dashawn…" She winced when he penetrated her ass.

"Shit. Relax Rachel it won't hurt as much if you relax" he panted as he stroked her slowly.

"Bullshit, I feel like I'm a stuffed turkey and there isn't any room to add more dressing. What in the hell? Shit, matter of fact that's what I won't be doing any more if you keep going," she ranted as he continued to slowly stroke in and out.

Dashawn tried to fight the need to laugh. "I promise it gets better if you relax your muscles. Relax," he urged.

Rachel decided to listen and once she began to relax, the feelings of pleasure began to fill her. She started moving with him and enjoyed the tight feeling that it provided, and each stroke hit her g-spot in a way that she lost thoughts for a second. Before long, she found herself backing into him in fast movements meeting him stroke for stroke. The deeper he went, the wetter she became, and the tight feeling became pure enjoyment. While she might not allow him to take her this way every time, she would permit him access occasionally.

"Thank you for taking this chance with me and not bucking me off of you when it was unbearable," he whispered.

"Thank you for meeting me for lunch Chelly," Lee told her when she sat down across from him a few months after the wedding.

"You don't have to thank me, Dad, we both agreed to put forth effort in repairing our relationship, and I meant that. I'm sorry I haven't been able to meet up for lunch sooner, the boys have kept me pretty busy." She smiled as she thought of her twin boys who'd just turned a year old.

"Those little rascals keep all of us busy I can't believe they're a year old already. They seem to be as busy as you were at their age. Thanks for the pictures and videos, it helps me feel a part of their lives even when I'm not there."

"Again, no need for thanks. You're their Pop Pop and they adore you. So, what's new?"

"Well, I uh-had a talk with Nisha, and she wanted me to apologize to you on her behalf. She now realizes the error of her ways. She understands if you don't accept it or anything, but Nate was very upset with her for ruining his chances of meeting you, causing them to have a fall out as well. I'm not sure what's going on with her these days and have suggested she figure it out before she winds up further hurt."

"I don't harbor any ill-feelings towards her, but I'm not interested in reconciling with her. While the boys are wonderful, I can't help but think about how they were born prematurely due to her antics. I'm sorry that Nate was a casualty, but I'm just not interested in a relationship with them yet. I don't know that I ever will be really, and I need for you to be okay with my decision. It doesn't change the fact that I want to have a relationship with you, but they've had you their whole lives. While I've been fighting for a morsel of time all of mine. I just want to be with you without interruption…." she paused looking at him with pleading eyes.

"If that's what you need, then that's what it'll be. I'm enjoying our time together even though we need to do better about our lunch dates. Maybe next time we can have lunch with the munchkins?" He smiled.

"Yeah and neither of us will get to eat because we'll be busy keeping them from destroying the restaurant."

"We'll see. I trust those two to behave with Pop Pop."

"Pop Pop, done lost his damn mind if he thinks one-year-old twin boys will listen and behave in a restaurant but ok. That's cute," she sarcastically replied.

Three hours later when she was at home, Dashawn asked, "So, how was your lunch with your father? Were you able to finish that report before you left work?"

"Jayden get down from there. Aiden, you better not throw that!" she yelled at the twins who were demolishing the other room.

"Did you hear me, Love?"

"No, your damn sons are destroying the living room, and I'm wondering who I made mad in my former life to warrant twins, thus giving me double fucking trouble…" She sighed.

"Double fucking trouble," the boys parroted.

"See, that's why I told you not to cuss around them. They're mini sailors who only recite curse words. And in perfect pitch, I might add." Dashawn shook his head.

"I keep forgetting that in this day and time in our lives that spelling is how we should communicate. This is bull-crap, I almost did it again. Boys!" She ranted.

"If you want to finish this, I'll get them," he told her as he stirred the pot on the stove.

"Humph, that'll mean that instead of them destroying the living room, I'll have to pick up their bedroom when you allow them to take every single toy out of the chest while you watch. No thanks. Let me see if they'll watch Moana. I'll be back, and you can remind me what it was you asked or said." Rachel walked into the living room smiling at her sons, happy with the course of her life. She loved being a mother despite having busybody twins…. it made her appreciate the journey her life had taken to get where she was.

EPILOGUE

Two years later...

Sitting in the lobby of Dr. Montgomery's office caused Dashawn some excitement as they waited. He hoped that everything was okay. "How are you feeling today Love?"

"Fat and pregnant."

Walking into the exam, he smiled at the nurse which made Rachel elbow him an, "Oomph, what the fuck?"

Rachel just glared at him as the nurse instructed her to climb on the table and told her the doctor would be right in.

"Is there a reason you elbowed me?" he snapped.

"I'm pregnant and you're grinning at women and shit," she ranted rolling her eyes.

"I was being polite and speaking," he told her as the doctor entered.

"Hey, you two so looks like we're going through another pregnancy. How're the boys? Rachel, this is gonna be cold." Dr. Montgomery made small talk while spreading the goo over her stomach.

"Yeah. Fine," Rachel one word answered.

"Excuse Mrs. Crabby, the boys are great and getting big, and boy are they busy," Dashawn responded.

"Oh, looky here. Uh well, Dashawn you uh-Hmmph…" Dr. Montgomery staggered.

"Is something wrong?" Rachel asked looking at the doctor after staring at her husband.

"N-nothing's wrong, I hate to tell you but looks like you're having another set of twins," she announced.

"Son of a fucking bitch! You've got to be shitting me, gotdamn, motherfucking cock sucker. Dashawn gotdamn Sanders!" Rachel screamed and hollered. "I'm going to kill your ass and slice open your twin making dick! What the entire fuck?"

"I do shit right…" He shrugged cockily.

"Really? You gonna be cocky right now? I'm not fucking you again. I bet you won't be cocky then."

"Yeah, and that's why you're in this situation now, my boys store up for the winter when you keep them from their home. How many more twins you want?"

"In that case, we fucking daily until one of us dies! I can't keep carrying twins, this is some bullshit."

Dr. Montgomery laughed at their banter, confirmed their due date and left the room tickled.

"Come on, so we can make do on that proposition. Practice makes perfect, Love."

"Fucking bullshit," she grumbled climbing off the table while cleaning her stomach.

Rachel still felt as if her life had moved in a positive direction as she pondered where she'd been in comparison to where she was now. She looked at the woman who'd started her towards her mend, ready to catch her up on things as she'd decreased her visits drastically once she got pregnant with Aiden and Jayden. "I'm happy that my life has evened out a little bit."

"I'd say so, how are you feeling?" Dr. Hawkins smiled at her.

"If I can keep that man off of me, I'd be ok. His damn sperm is potent, he seems to knock me up after time-lapsed sexual occurrences." Rachel smiled rubbing her growing baby bump.

"You might want to stop withholding from him for long periods of time then. How are you doing otherwise?" Dr. Hawkins teased.

"Shit, that's hard to do with a busy career and raising twins who are rambunctious. But considering this is my second set of twins, I think you're right. I think whenever he doesn't get it for a while his sperm has a team meeting, where they decide to make a lasting impact when they gain access again. They jumped my poor eggs with gusto forcing a double conception. These babies are gonna be identical as well, but unlike their brothers, they're refusing to show their gender. *Little Terrors*. Anyway, other than baby making, I'm doing well. Work is busy and quite fulfilling. Dashawn has been traveling a lot with his job, which is another reason we don't get to be intimate as often. I've also been trying to plan another *Girl's Trip* for my friends, cousin and I, but the timing may be off as my cousin Charlene is getting married to Quincy, not Mark. That in itself is a funny story and concept because I never expected it to happen.

Oh, and my friends, Kayla and Caressa are expecting again," she finished smiling with excitement.

"Wow, that's a lot at once. I'm so happy to hear that, and I want you to remember something as you go along on your journey, since you don't seem to need me anymore. The first thing is, if things get to be too much, I'm just a phone call away. I also want you to remember this, you might think you don't matter in this world, but because of you, someone hears a song on the radio, and it reminds them of you. Someone has read a book you recommended to them and gotten lost in its pages. Someone's remembered a joke you told them and smiled to themselves. Someone's tried on an outfit and felt beautiful because you complimented them on it. Someone has a memory that makes them grin as it involves you. Someone now likes themselves that little bit more because you made a passing comment that made them feel good. Never think you don't have an impact, your fingerprints can't be wiped away from the little marks of kindness that you've left behind. Someone has been impacted and changed because of you. Your life has been meaningful and rewarding to someone you don't even know."

Rachel stood up and wrapped her arms around Dr. Hawkins as tears streamed from her eyes. She'd been an asset in her healing and she knew that if she ever needed her, she would be available to her. "Thank you for those impactful words. I will remember them and call you if I need some reassurance," she said stepping out of the embrace.

"Hey Chelly, I was heading over to see the boys, are you home?" her father asked when she answered her phone moments after exiting Dr. Hawkins' office.

"Hey Dad, no I'm not home, but the boys are there with Dashawn if you want to go over still. I'll give him a call to let him know you're coming," she told him.

"Ok, cool. I'll see you when you get home. Love you."

"No problem. Love you too Dad. See you later," she said hanging up then calling Dashawn. "Hi babe," she greeted when he picked up.

"Hi Love, how'd your session go today?" he asked.

"It went very well. Uh, I'm heading over to see Kayla, but my dad is on his way over to see the boys. I hope that's ok? I should be there after a while."

"Not a problem at all, we're sitting here watching TV. I'm sure the boys will enjoy a visit from Pop Pop," he said causing the boys to scream excitedly.

"Yeah, sounds like it. See you guys later, babe. Love you."

"Alright, until then. Love you more, Love."

Dashawn watched Aiden and Jayden tackle Lee with roars and growls. He loved his family. Talking to his wife a little bit ago let him know that she was in a good place which pleased him immensely. It seemed like ever since the boys were born she had a reason to live more than before. She was a great mother…he loved the way she mothered their children. He couldn't wait to see what awaited them as the parents of two sets of twins. He laughed as he remembered her reaction to the news. Calling him cocky and ranting like a madwoman.

Dashawn loved Rachel and all the flaws that she showed as well as the ones she hid. Nothing would change his mind. The decision to make his would-be one-night-stand permanent in his life was the best decision of his life. He had absolutely no regrets whatsoever.

After a couple hours, he put the boys to bed they were tired after spending the afternoon playing with Rachel's dad. He walked back into the living room where he'd left Rachel sitting on the couch. He tapped on his phone a few times until he found what he was searching for. Then he walked over to her extending his hand. "Dance with me, Love."

"I can't dance with all of this in front of me, are you kidding? We won't even be able to get close," she grumbled as she rubbed her stomach.

"Sure, we can, we'll take it slow." He helped her up from the couch and paused to turn off the lights letting the hall light be their beacon.

"Thank you for being you Dashawn and loving me the way that you do…" she started as they began two-stepping to the song.

You say you love me, lady...girl, I hope you do...only you can save me...my life equals you...kiss me, drive me crazy...would you do that for me, lady?...

"I've got you always, Love. No thanks are EVER needed," he said as he spun her slowly around. Her happiness was his desire, and it pleased him to give her what she needed. As he told her many times before, he had her for the rest of her life and what a life it would be. *Love...complete and whole is the sweetest reward after devastation, and it pleasures me to provide it to her even when she doesn't feel deserving or worthy of it.*

THE END

ABOUT THE AUTHOR

Riley Baxter is a new author from Ohio. Being new to the writing scene, she is hopeful that her debut novel, ***Meeting Dr. Feelgood*** and her second Novel, ***Saving Rachel*** will have readers flocking to Amazon searching for future releases. As she continues to write as a form of escape, she looks forward to readers tapping into her wild imagination and journeys toward a happily ever after. When not writing, she can be categorized as an introvert with a passion and love for reading and escaping life with the help of her favorite authors.

Saving Rachel is Riley Baxter's second Novel. See Her Debut Novel, ***Meeting Dr. Feelgood*** and read how the characters in Saving Rachel met.